T0121290

DEMONS IN COLD WATER

MAC MUZVIMWE

authorHOUSE®

AuthorHouse™ UK
1663 Liberty Drive
Bloomington, IN 47403 USA
www.authorhouse.co.uk
Phone: 0800.197.4150

© *2015 Mac Muzvimwe. All rights reserved.*

No part of this book may be reproduced, stored in a retrieval system, or transmitted by any means without the written permission of the author.

Published by AuthorHouse   01/12/2016

ISBN: 978-1-5049-9469-9 (sc)
ISBN: 978-1-5049-9470-5 (hc)
ISBN: 978-1-5049-9471-2 (e)

Print information available on the last page.

Any people depicted in stock imagery provided by Thinkstock are models, and such images are being used for illustrative purposes only. Certain stock imagery © Thinkstock.

This book is printed on acid-free paper.

Because of the dynamic nature of the Internet, any web addresses or links contained in this book may have changed since publication and may no longer be valid. The views expressed in this work are solely those of the author and do not necessarily reflect the views of the publisher, and the publisher hereby disclaims any responsibility for them.

to Devon & Kristian:
"stars are made to shine"

CHAPTER ONE

—⊶⊷—

1 Mist hung in the purple shades of the evening. Loud bangs could be heard in the distance. Isolated flickering lights accentuated the darkness. Eli wondered what was better; the crispy mist or the humid rain which had fallen incessantly for the past four days. He decided the mist was better as he pushed the half-glass door. It swung open, and he stood at the door for a moment with a sense of hesitation. The bar was nearly empty. It was long and narrow, with poor lighting. The bar counter and stools were painted a dingy cream. In fact, all the furniture was that colour. At the stage, there was a mediocre band playing. Of course, it sounded more karaoke than anything else. It was after a full minute that Eli decided to enter. He supposed that at least it was warmer, and probably much safer than the dark streets of Jerusalem.

"Lemonade, please," he said to the burly barman.
"Full or half?" responded the barman in a husky voice with a strong Arabic accent.

"A full pint, please. With a lemon, but no ice."

"No lemon, ice no, ok? Yes, no?" said the barman seemingly rather annoyed at Eli's request.

Eli turned his attention to the stage. There was a pretty girl singing a cover version of Bill Monroe's *"The One I Love is Gone"*. Eli's eyes stalked the pretty girl. She had half-cut hair, and even with the poor lighting, he could see her beautiful face. The only spotlight which shone above the stage made her beautiful skin seem translucently orange. He watched her lips as they sung soulfully. Her mouth was a crimson promise. Eli had not looked at a girl that way since the first time he saw Zahara. That seemed like a lifetime ago. Of course, it was. Seventeen years, four months and eleven days to be exact. Even when he met her in a fragile state, Zahara still looked alluring, bold and beautiful, and her eyes dazzled with audacity.

This girl also had a sweet infectious voice that, for some reason, reminded him of a TV commercial that aired mainly around the Christmas season.

"Well I found the bluebird; High on a mountainside;
And the little bird would sing its little song
So I'll sigh, I'll cry; I'll even want to die
For the one I love is gone"

He knew the song very well. It was one of his favourite songs. It captured everything that he had felt many times in his life.

For a moment, Eli got lost in his thoughts. He only came back when a couple of people clapped to signal end of the song. He clapped too. He kept clapping even after everyone else had stopped. Then he watched the girl coming down the stairs. He quickly turned his head and gazed thoughtlessly at his glass of lemonade.

"Get it together, you are thirty-eight for goodness' sake," he silently cursed himself. "She is only a girl. Only girl, and she is not Zahara; besides, you are married now."

He stood up and walked from the bar counter. He found an empty table in the far corner. The light above it flickered after every few seconds. He sat there and pulled his journal, and started writing, immediately forgetting about the singing girl. He was in Jerusalem to find redemption, and not to court women. He was there to find himself before it was too late. He was there to save his marriage.

Before he could write anything in his journal, he heard a female voice say in a fluent and neutral accent, "Hi there. A penny for your thoughts; mind if I join you?"

"Why?" Eli responded after casting a quick glance at her, before pretending to read something in his journal. It was the singing girl.

"That's rather unexpected. There I thought you were good company," she said as she pulled a chair to sit.

"Um, actually I do mind," he said. "I am trying to write something, so I really need to be by myself."

"Oh dear, aren't you rather curt?" she said, seating herself down anyway.

He cast another glance at her as she sat down. She was pretty. He looked at her auburn hair. It was nice but he could immediately tell that it was not her natural colour. She had almond eyes; very big and sparkly.

"I am Mary," she said offering her hand.

"You didn't even listen to a word I said, did you?" he asked sarcastically but with a broad smile. "I am Joseph," he added and felt rather pleased with that response. A whimsical smile ran across his lips.

"Why would you lie to a pretty girl like me, especially with those beautiful teeth?" she giggled.

"Oh, I thought we were playing some kind of allegorical game; you are Mary and I am Joseph, and we are in Jerusalem. Start with the truth, and then maybe, only maybe, we can have a real conversation."

"Who made a cranky tourist out of you? Let me see if I can pacify you. What makes you say Mary is not my real name? What makes you think I am not being truthful?"

"Look at yourself. How old are you? Twenty-what? Now ask me how old I am. I am not your sort of company, now am I? Either you are trying to play some twisted game with me or you enjoy prying on innocent strangers. So, I will ask again, what can I do for you? I am usually a nice guy but I really must do my writing."

She toyed with him a bit longer, with words full of wicked deception up to a point when the annoyance started to show on Eli's face.

For as long as she could remember, all boys wanted her. Even her father wanted her. Not a day went by without her thinking about her horrible father. Not a day went by without her cursing her beauty. For if it was not for her beauty, she knew for certain she would have led a different life.

It had been raining on the night of her escape. It was the night her father kicked into her room. It was a week before she was due to be handed over for marriage to a man more than three times her age. He stood framed against the ashen light in her bedroom. She could see that his zipper was open, and his manhood stood out. She was only thirteen. Unlucky thirteen, she often said. She remembers muttering to herself "why me?" He was shirtless, and she could see the greasy hair on his chest. She could hear her mother whimpering in the next room. He went straight for her and pushed her onto her single bed. His rough hands tore off her white blouse, as they searched for her little budding breasts. Her whole body shivered in fear. She closed her eyes and thought about praying, but a thought told her it was better to die fighting instead. She raised her left arm and searched for her scissors, but she could not find it. She felt him heaving towards her, with his nails digging into her flesh, frantically tearing at her underwear. Her left arm tried again. Searched, and searched until it eventually found. She found the scissors. Without thought and with all her budding teenage feminine power, she thrust into his neck, just under his left ear. She heard him roar in agony. She felt warm liquid ooze out. She pushed him over. She grabbed her school dress from the dressing table. She cast her eyes on him, and saw him writhing in pain. She picked up her makeshift cricket bat and went for his manhood. He screamed. He tried to say something but no words came out. She put on her school dress, searched for another pair of pants and some shoes. She quickly shoved a few items of clothing into her rucksack. She went to her mother in the next room, and found her sitting in the corner with puffy eyes. She wanted to kick her too for failing to protect her but she felt a sense of sadness; they were both victims. She felt sorry for her. She leaned over and kissed her, and muttered "I love you" in Yemeni Arabic and left. She never looked back.

"I am serious now, I do not have time for games. I have some issues to attend to," retorted Eli. "You seem to be kind of popular, so why are you bothering me? Are you not satisfied with the current attention you are getting?"

Sensing his growing frustration, she decided to stop being flippant. "Look around sweetheart. If I was popular, would I be playing in this dump? I am just looking for good company in this godforsaken shithole. I travel a lot, and yes, it does get lonely sometimes, so excuse me for looking for a friendly face." She stood up to leave.

"Ok," he said slowly with tension on his face thawing again, "I am Elijah, but I prefer Eli." He felt rather bad for his earlier outburst. He let a broad smile parade his neatly arranged teeth, for he always knew he had a beautiful smile. Zahara always said it oozed out heartfelt sincerity.

"I like you. You have a sense of mystery. You are not from here, and you do not look like the typical tourist," she said as she sat down again. "Otherwise, you would be nowhere near this area, especially at this time of the night. Normal tourists flock to West Jerusalem. So, yes, you intrigue me. By the way, I also write, um, I am a journalist, so I am always looking for interesting untold stories."

Eli had no answer to that. So, she continued, "Let me go and get a drink, and we can talk."

He watched her walk away. He liked the curve of her hips. She did not have long legs like Zahara, but he thought they were long enough. She returned moments later with a cup of frosted coffee.

"The coffee here is shit, yet I drink it anyway. The trick is to overload it with sugar, just a little bit," she said and chortled.

She did not expect Eli to respond, so she continued "Ok, let's talk, Eli. So, are you named after the biblical Elijah, the one with the chariots of fire?" she chortled again. "When I tell you my name, you will be the first one to know it in over fourteen years. Surely that must count for something."

"No offence, but I am not asking you to trust me with anything. Like I said, I have my own issues to attend to. If you want your name to be Mary, then Mary it is," he scoffed lightly.

"Why are you so frosty? Most men would welcome the tranquil company of a beautiful woman. What are you doing here, anyway? I mean here in Jerusalem."

"You said 'most men', so I do not have to justify why I am in the other group, do I? What do most people come to Jerusalem to do? To find redemption, I guess; I don't know, something like that."

"Ok, I am Kaela, daughter of a Yemeni father and a Turkish mum, grew up in a small village in Syria near the border with Turkey," she paused and looked across the table. "Um, Kaela means sweetheart, that's why I am such a sweetheart," she giggled again before continuing. "Your turn, so which part of the Western world do you hail from?"

"What makes you think I am a Westerner?" Eli asked with a capricious smile and trying to distort his accent.

"Well, many things. Your accent is certainly not from here, your skin tone indicates a colder climate, your clothes, your watch… shall I continue? I told you I have a good observational eye. I have met many people in my years of travel. You will be amazed how easy it is to derive a few facts by merely looking at someone."

"I'm from South Africa, but have been living in Britain for the past nine years, so maybe that explains the accent. The watch was a gift from a friend in Australia, so that explains nothing."

"Cool. Can I say cool, or that's too avant-garde for you?" she teased. "How about we continue this conversation somewhere decent? I know a few nice restaurants that open late and do half-decent meals. It's all on me, and I could even become your tourist guide if you stop being mean. Teach how to build bridges rather than just burn them."

"Just say you want to have your way with me," joked Eli. "There is nothing called a free dinner."

Kaela sniggered, and the drink gagged in her throat. She immediately put the glass down, and slapped a hand to her mouth and swallowed distraughtly.

"Ooh, that's so unladylike," Eli added as tears of choking laughter sprung to Kaela's eyes. "I am a high class gigolo, so you're going to have to do better than that if you want to have your way with me!"

She drove a neat two-door Mercedes coupe. She headed towards Western Jerusalem, and drove up to a nice restaurant on the top of hill, with views looking over the West Bank.

"This is the best view to watch all the shelling of the poor Palestinians by their masters, whilst rich tourists sit here and drink their expensive sherry," she said rather mordantly with a stern look on her face.

They were seated in the corner booth. It was still raining, so the outside tables were deserted. She ordered a beef burger, rare, and she chuckled, "So, I like Western food, big deal. I am famished after belting my voice in that dump."

"Why do you sing in that dump anyway?" asked Eli, as he cut through his oversized piece of well-done sirloin steak.

"I have always wanted to sing, but you heard my voice, I am no Broadway material. Besides, as a journalist you can get lots of information about anything, you know, the real news, uncensored in dumps like that."

"Just say you love the thrill of those drunk fucks gazing at you," Eli chided lightly, before regretting saying a swear word. "Pardon my unholy language."

"I caught you gazing too, Eli, didn't I? And you were not even drunk!"

"Touché, nicely done" smiled Eli and could not hide that he was warming up to her. She sensed it too.

They conversed throughout their meal, sharing a few jokes and warming up to each other. Eli felt at ease with this girl. He had not had a meaningful conversation since leaving London two months earlier. His plan was to stay for another five weeks, and then return home to Scarlett and their two girls, April and Skye. The self-imposed exile was a design to help fight the demons from the days past.

"So, where do you want to go now, Mr Tourist?" asked Kaela. "The night is young; it's only just gone eleven o'clock."

"I am not much of a night person. I could do with going back to my hotel now. Relax, take a bath, write some more, I don't know. I think I have had enough, and thank you for your hospitality. Sorry, I do not know how to say 'thank you' in Hebrew."

"It's *'toda lach'* when you say it to a female, *'toda lecha'* if to a male. But to keep it simple, just say *'toda raba'*. I hate Hebrew, so I do not use it unless I have to. Anyway, you are welcome, old man. Now, let's take you to bed before you get delirious," she teased. "Where are you staying?"

"My hotel is on the other side of the district heading towards Beit Shemesh, do you know that area well?"

"Of course, I do. Sadly, I know every square inch of this place. I have suite on the opposite side, come with me for a cup of tea or something? Aren't you British people supposed to love tea? I know, I know… you are British by residence, so calm down! Surely, you must be able to stay a bit late, it's not like you have to work tomorrow."

"My itinerary says I have a busy day planned for tomorrow," he lied unconvincingly. Kaela sniggered, and mockingly did a sad puppy face as she got up to leave. Eli did not say a word, he just smiled and followed. As he shut the door, Kaela said, "You said you are here to fight your demons." It was a more of a statement than a question. She reached into her glove compartment, and pulled out an Oxford English mini-dictionary. "Demon, demon, D… ah, here it is. Demon – a devil or evil spirit, and um, a cruel, evil, forceful or destructive person or thing. So, what voodoo spirits or destructive thing or person are you fighting, Eli?" she asked as she put back the dictionary.

"Aren't you full of questions," said Eli as he turned to look at her. "Come on drive, I will tell you. We all have demons, don't we? Some have more than others. Maybe I have had one too many demons or maybe I have a propensity for self-destruction but life is a game of inches, so here's to inching towards redemption."

CHAPTER TWO

‹━⦿⦿⦿━›

2 Self-destruction or not, Eli always knew that his incessant passion for love lost would eventually be his downfall. And it was a battle that he had always known that he would never win, no matter how much he fought or how far he ran, but for the sake of his daughters, he wanted to try.

It was a hot April afternoon in Zimbabwe when he met her. He was on a six-month work secondment in Harare, rolling out the new procedures for security analysis, investment practice and statistical analyses. It was a good role for a 23-year old, just a year after finishing university and still working towards chartership. So, when the post was advertised at their office in Pretoria, he took it. For a lot of people, Zimbabwe was a shithole where people were being robbed, mugged and raped by the politicians' thugs. But he thought it could not be any worse than what was happening in the Johannesburg slums. "Same shit, different towns," he had said to his mum when he told her. Besides, the secondment pay was very good. He was going to use it put down a deposit for his first house or apartment. He knew that would make his mum proud; a house at 23 years of age but the truth was that he desperately needed time away from his High School sweetheart. He had been with Scarlett since he was sixteen. He knew she was a good girl, but he often told his friends that he would rather leave her than cheat on her. It was not that he was bursting with lust or infatuation, but he justified it in his young mind that he just wanted a change of scenery and six months in Harare offered him just that. It was a good opportunity for him to free himself for a short while, and help him to rediscover his passion.

He saw her crying, walking barefooted down the lane next to the central park. He had seen many kids crying and walking down that same street but had never paid attention to them but this was different.

He had opted to drive around the avenues of Harare that afternoon. The morning session at work had taken a lot out of him. Old men with eyes full of contempt, hatred and scorn as they stared and listened to a young foreign boy telling them to change their ways of working; telling them new things which were hard to learn. Eli often emphasised to them that everyone had to do it or they risked "being left behind". They all knew that it meant "being fired". Who was this little boy still with pimples on his cheeks? The nerve of the corporate bosses in Pretoria to send a young boy to teach them. He knew they all hated him. He did not understand the local Shona language, but he knew they were cursing him. Normally, it did not faze him. During his school years and all the way to university, he had always been top of the class, so he was used to being envied and despised in equal proportions, but his mom always told him his brains were God's gift, and he ought to embrace that gift fully.

But for some reason, the session of that particular Friday morning took a lot out of him. He had heard someone mutter at the end of the session, "You are lucky we do not know your totem, otherwise, we would set voodoo on your diaper-covered bottom." The thought of someone openly wanting to harm him made his whole body quiver with fear. He still had another month to go before returning back to South Africa.

When Eli saw her walking down that lane, he immediately noticed her long brown legs skimpily covered by tomato-red denim shorts, before moving his eyes up to her long black hair with weave-on extensions. His loins instantly lusted for her legs. Even from a distance, they looked silk smooth. They were the kind that he always fantasised wrapped around his waist. He muttered under his breath, "Whoa, mama". He initially drove past her, but when he looked in his rear view mirror, he saw that she was crying. It was only then that he noticed that she was not wearing any shoes. He screeched to a halt, parked his car and walked towards her.

"Hi, are you ok? Sorry I can't speak Shona, can you understand me?" he asked with a genuinely sympathetic tone.

She did not say a word. She nodded her head, and kept walking.

"My name is Eli. Are you ok? Come on, let's sit down on that bench in the park. Maybe I can help," he said as he lightly touched her hand.

She stopped walking, as she wiped off the tears off her eyes and some snort from her nose. Eli took out some soft tissue paper from his jacket and handed her some. She took them, and offered the unused ones back after wiping herself, but Eli gestured her to keep them. She stared at his eyes for a long moment. He smiled, intentionally trying to exude sincerity. Ever since he was a kid, his smile had always been his get-out-of-jail card; he almost felt bad for using it on her. She turned without saying a word and walked towards the park bench. He followed her and sat on the bench. He did not say a word.

"Thank you," she said after about twenty minutes of silence and watching cars driving by.

"You are welcome. I am just trying to help. Anyway, I have to go back to work now, my lunch break finished a few minutes ago. It's not that I really want to go back to work. Everyone hates me but being late would only aggravate matters," he shared with a smile.

She looked at him and forced a dim smile. She got up first. Eli remained seated and looked at her from toe to head, and thought, "Dear God, who would make such a pretty girl cry?" She had eyes that sparkled with a ray of blue like sapphire. Her hair cascaded around her face like a halo of black diamonds. Her lips looked soft and tender, and Eli thought he would give anything to kiss them. For a moment, Eli was lost in his own thoughts of awe, amazement and fantasy.

"My name is Zahara," she said. She pronounced her words clearly, and her accent sounded different to what Eli had gotten accustomed during his stay in Harare.

He got up too, and gestured her to walk with him towards his car. He took out a wad of cash from his wallet and gave it to her, as his eyes ran up and down her body one more time. She wore a tight white body-top which accentuated the swell of her breasts. The denim shorts showed the full curves of her slender hips and the brown of her long legs. Eli felt like a heartless pervert for lusting after a poor girl seemingly in trouble.

"I don't know what's happening with you, but hope that helps. It's not a lot but it should be enough for you to stay at a hotel for a couple of days, and maybe some extra clothes and shoes," he said as Zahara hesitated accepting the money. Eli continued, "Hey, look, I am not some sick pervert or stalker. Just want to help. All you have to do is take the money and walk away, and maybe say thank you."

Zahara accepted the money, and walked a few steps back with her eyes firmly cast on him. "Why?" she asked. "I do not even remember your name? Why are you helping me? Do you want sex from me? You sit with me for half an hour, say nothing and you leave a bundle of cash, and still want nothing from me?" She paused for a while and asked again, "Why?" She started crying again. Eli took her left hand, and spoke softly, "Look Zahara, I am just being nice. If you believe in God, then say I am your angel for today. If you do not believe in God, then just say this is your lucky day and thank your lucky stars." He released her hand, and patted her on the back, and walked away.

"Wait," shouted Zahara. She walked over to Eli, and hugged him as she whispered "Thank you."

Eli took a business card from his wallet, and handed it to her. "Those are my South African contact details. But on the back is my mobile phone number for here. I am here for another month or so, just in case you need anything else. Bye, and good luck." He walked to his car and got in. He started the engine and hesitated for a moment. He rolled down the window and said to her, "Just so I don't regret not saying this to you. You are the prettiest girl I have ever seen." With that he drove away. Zahara stared at the foreign number plates on his car, and thought they looked weird. Inside the car, Eli grinned and hoped that the undefined moment they had shared would last for as long as he needed it to.

Chapter Three

3 It took approximately twenty minutes to get to Kaela's hotel, and by the time they got there, the rain was pounding down intensely. The hotel lobby had lots of artefacts from different parts of the world. One of the pieces reminded Eli of the mosque that he used drive past everyday on his way to work back home in England.

They took the stairs to Kaela's suite on the first floor. As they entered, Eli admired the hardwood floor, and thought it looked exquisite. The room was panelled in solid rosewood, and the eastern wall was covered by a huge map of the world. On the opposite end was a huge glass-topped black oak desk in front of a large window. He knew a little bit about construction from his construction trades classes in secondary school. His father was also a civil engineer. The thought of his father made him flinch involuntarily. Luckily, he paid no further mind to him because Kaela yelled something at him.

"Sorry, what did you say?" he asked.

"I said make yourself comfortable," she responded as she made her way into the bathroom.

"How can you afford such a place? You must be writing good articles. That's pretty impressive for a freelance journo," remarked Eli and went on to tease "Or maybe it's money from your singing career?"

"Hey, I make decent money once in a while, and I have zero responsibilities, that's why I can afford a few luxuries. Besides, those 'drunk fucks' you mentioned from that bar, they tip very well," she said as she walked out of the bathroom. She had slipped into a beige silk gown, and had a white towel around her hair. "Hey, stop lusting after me, you dirty strange man," she teased as a smile lit up her face. It caught Eli by surprise; he had not noticed that he had been staring at her.

Ten minutes later, they sat on the couch drinking some exotic herbal tea gently conversing like old friends. Their instant chemistry astonished Eli, but he had been down that road before. He also knew that if he was to successfully redeem his troubled soul and save his marriage, he had to shake off distractions like Kaela. "The road to redemption has no GPS," he thought quietly but with visible vigour on his face as if he was debating with someone. But deep inside he knew he was just rationalising his thoughts.

"What are you grimacing about?" asked Kaela.
"Oh, sorry, did that show?" said Eli rather embarrassed, "It's something I read but I can't remember where I read it. It was a statement that said 'the road to redemption has no GPS'."

"Interesting. It kind of makes sense though, doesn't it? Anyway, tell me more about your demons and the redemption you so need."

"Hey, I have said enough for today; it's your turn," Eli responded.

"Next time, I will be the talker," she said.

"There will be a next time?" Eli asked rhetorically. "What's with you and wanting to know? You want to feed on my misery and gauge how messed up I am? Or are you doing a human story for your next article?"

"Ha, ha, I am more fucked up than you in many ways. Trust me. Yours seems just like a sad love story to me. All I have heard so far is about a crush on a girl," she teased again and continued, "So, what happened with the girl? Did you ever see her again, or you still rue the missed opportunity?"

"Ok, you don't give up, do you? Of course, I saw her again," he sighed and chuckled, "a year or so later."

Chapter Four

4 Eli walked briskly from the elevator. He felt quite guilty for taking more than the stipulated one hour for lunch. He walked briskly past the reception desk in hope that the receptionist would not notice him.

"Eli, slow down," said the receptionist. Eli turned back and smiled at her wryly, "What I can do for you, sweetness?"

"Well, for one, you could have taken me to lunch with you. Seriously though, Thando has been complaining about people taking longer lunch breaks."

"Oh shit! Is she in? It won't happen again. Did she say something about me?" asked Eli.

"Well, let's discuss it over dinner," laughed the receptionist and continued when she realised Eli was not going to respond. "She has not said anything about you yet, but she has asked me to start taking note of serial offenders." As Eli turned to go, she signalled to him that there was more. Eli rolled his eyes as he walked back to her. "I am serious about lunch or dinner. Come to my flat for a nice home-cooked…"

"Hey, Eli, my man, there is a nice piece of ass in your office," interrupted a rather raucous voice coming from a man about Eli's age, as he passed through the reception area.

"Big mouth Fred," said the receptionist trying to hide her disappointment at the interruption. "I was about to tell him. Don't you have a job to do you uncultured swine?"

Eli left the two arguing and headed to his office. He had no idea who was in his office. It was a short walk to his office. He opened the door and quickly cast his eyes over to the visitor's chair, and for a moment, he was lost for words.

"Hi Eli," said Zahara. "I see you are surprised, I hope pleasantly so." She remained seated.

Eli did not know whether to shake her hand or bend over to hug her. He had dreamed about her many times. The encounter at the park had played in his mind many times. He had thought about the many ways things could have panned out. He was convinced he would never see her again. It had been just over a whole year since the day he saw her. So, he was lost for emotion when he saw her sitting there, smiling beautifully at him. He wanted to embrace her. He wanted to tell her that he loved her. He wanted to do things to her that he had fantasised about many times over. Many times in his head he had recalled how beautiful she had looked that afternoon. He often wondered whether his fondness of that mystery girl in the park exaggerated her actual beauty. He once told the story to a colleague, who in response had remarked "Get hold of yourself Eli, no one is that beautiful." He was wrong. She radiated with beauty; every part of her was beautiful.

"If it's a bad time, I will come back another time, Eli," she said as she stood up. "But in all fairness, I have been waiting for nearly an hour."

Eli grabbed her hand, and said, "I am sorry for my loss of words, but you have no idea what this means. How did you find me? What are you doing in Pretoria? You look really beautiful. Would you like to go for a late lunch?"

"I am happy that you are happy to see me," she smiled again and remained standing. "Haven't you just come back from lunch? Thanks for offering but I am fine."

"Give me two minutes," said Eli and left the office.

He returned a short while later, and said "Come on, let's get out of here. I have said there is a family emergency."

As the pair of them walked down the hallway, Eli knew the prying eyes of his work colleagues were peering through the blinds. He did not care. He was the happiest he had ever been.

They took Eli's car and drove to the suburban parts of the city while Zahara did most of the talking. She spoke of how much she had thought about him and how peculiar it was that he helped her and never asked for anything in return. She told him that he saved her life that day.

"How so?" asked Eli.

"I can't tell you the details but you did. I thought about that encounter many times, and even though I am not religious, I wholly believe that on that day you were God-sent. If there is anything I can ever do for you, please just let me know," she paused and patted him. "I could start by buying you dinner this evening."

"Just seeing you, just knowing that you thought of me is enough for me. Sounds corny but it's true. As for dinner, I am not bothered, I just want to be somewhere where we can just converse some more to be honest. Anyway, how long are you in Pretoria for?"

"That's the good part. I moved down here about six weeks ago. I have a modelling contract for two years, so I have a flat in Sunnyside."

Eli could not believe what he was hearing. The wide grin on his mouth spoke of his delight.

"Judging by that wide grin, you must really like me," joked Zahara.

"You have no idea how much I love you," blurted out Eli. He regretted it the moment the words left his lips. He wanted to hide. He felt like he had ruined the moment.

"You couldn't possibly love me. I am sure you are just excited to see me. I am too," smiled Zahara as she stroked his hand. Eli smiled back and did not say anything. He was sure he loved her but he figured why ruin the moment again. Even if he had not said it, he would still have felt it so there was really not much sense in not saying it. The instant connection to her was overwhelming.

They eventually drove to Zahara's apartment in Sunnyside. It was a spacious two bedroom flat on the third floor, with ultra-modern furnishings. Paintings of famous cities concealed the upper section of the white and red wallpaper.

"I am sorry. Eli, I am a bad cook. Are you ok with fried rice? That's all I can do."

"Let's make something together. I make a brilliant beef stir-fry. It's my mother's speciality."

"You just want to show off, don't you? Don't worry, I am easily impressionable," laughed Zahara as she patted him rather sensually on the back. Eli thought to himself either she was a touchy-feely person or she really liked him too.

They enjoyed a quiet evening, and chatted into the late hours about a wide range of general issues. Zahara listened intently with her eyes firmly gazed on him as he talked about his family. He showed emotion and vulnerability when he spoke about how he hated his father for leaving him and his mom when he was three. He wanted to tell her about how hurt he was when his estranged father returned for a short while many years later and his mother took him back seemingly with no questions asked. Now his mom and his seven-year old brother were struggling with AIDS. He wanted to pour out everything but thought better of it. He did not know how long he had with her; he had to make the best of the time than seek sympathy.

"Families are complicated," that's all Zahara said on the subject, and got up to go to the kitchen. She came back with two cups of herbal tea.

"It's good for your skin, so don't you say no," she said as she handed one of the cups to Eli. Eli smiled before taking a sip. She continued, "I still do not understand why you helped me, Eli? How come you did not want anything in return? You just gave me some money and walked away. I never told anyone about it because I knew no one would ever believe me. It is one of those moments that I know for certain I will never experience again, so every now and again, when I close my eyes, I remember it all again."

"I don't know to be honest. You looked so sincere... so fragile, desperate and lost, and I just wanted to help. So if I had asked for something in return, I would have looked like every other perverted male, wouldn't I? You were just so sweet. Maybe, if you were not so pretty, I would not have helped. It doesn't matter; the great thing is that you are fine now. Besides, what would you have given me in return?" asked Eli and laughed awkwardly

As soon as Eli stopped talking, Zahara pulled the mug from Eli's hand, and leaned forward to kiss him. She kissed him for a few seconds, and then moved back. She took off her clothes slowly and teasingly. Eli remained motionless staring up her curves. Her legs were exactly how he had imagined them; long and smooth. He shuddered at the thought of licking them slowly. She moved closer to him, and knelt down in front of him as she undid his belt. He lifted his bottom, and she pulled away his jeans trousers and boxers together. She stared at his throbbing penis. It was long and thick, with a curve to the left. She took hold of it, and slid it into her mouth. Eli gasped and closed his eyes. Exhilaration!

Moments later she stood up again. Eli tried to move forward but she gently pushed back into the lounge chair. She raised her left knee and slowed moved it outwards. Eli saw the dark, irregular cleft of her womanhood and the swell of its lips; big lips they were. Eli always said he wanted a woman with 'meaty curtains'. He closed his eyes. He could not hear anything else other than the beating of his own heart.

She propelled forward and rested her legs on the chair. She teasingly rubbed against Eli before guiding him in. He thrust upwards into the warm smooth fluid canal. She gasped and moaned, and closed her eyes. Eli moved forward and slowly stood up. He carried her slowly to the bedroom. He felt an explosion building within him. She whispered into his left ear, "Fuck me, senseless." He lips quivered. He knew he had to oblige. He could win or lose her with that first sexual encounter. He tried not to make himself anxious but he knew she was way out of his league; how could he not feel apprehensive. He also had not been with woman since Scarlett left six months earlier. He flooded his mind with non-sexual thoughts to make himself last longer. He bit his lower lip and thrust harder.

It lasted eleven minutes; he had been watching the clock next to the bed. Zahara put her long legs around his waist, and her arms around his back. She felt her own climax rising. Eli bent his head down, grasped her right breast and took it into his mouth. He suckled and rasped it with his tongue, gently biting it. She felt an explosion in her body. He pumped faster and deeper. She caressed Eli's back muscles before she dug in her nails. She screamed, "Eli." He pumped harder for another minute before he felt his own explosion running through his loins. He winced and groaned. He cried, "Oh babe," before collapsing on top of her.

They held on to each other until the final shiver of Eli's orgasm was gone. Then he rolled over to the side, and kissed her on the shoulder. He nibbled on her ear and softly whispered, "Just like heaven."

"I know," she whispered back as she stroked his chest. "Raindrops falling, and love angels beckoning," she added before letting out a short subtle laugh.

He stayed over for the night. It was Eli's happiest day. Zahara was only the second woman he had had sex with but he told himself he would never want another woman ever again.

He did not go to work the following day. He phoned the office and asked for compassionate day off on grounds of family issues.

They spent all morning in bed watching TV. Eli felt complete. In the afternoon, they drove to Johannesburg for shopping, and ended the day with dinner at a posh French restaurant in Sandton.

CHAPTER FIVE

5 "You look good, ma," Eli said he entered his mum's house and kissed her on the cheek. "Where is my little brother?" he yelled. Justin, his 7-year old brother, came dashing down the hallway and jumped on to him.

"Long time no see, big brother," said Justin.

"I am sorry, little brother, you know how it is," smiled Eli.

"Well, I don't know how it is. Anyway, did you bring me anything? You know I am on borrowed time," he said with a wide grin trying to guilt his older brother.

"Justin, what did I tell you about saying that?" complained Ma Zwide. "Talk to him, Eli, he has been saying that a lot to guilt people."

Eli did not respond to his mum. Inside, his heart was breaking. With each visit, he could see his innocent little brother wasting away. And with each visit, he hated his father more and more.

"Has he been around?" Eli asked his mum when Justin left the room.

"Do not let that bother you my son. I have forgiven him. In fact, there was nothing to forgive. I am the one who took him back but aren't we all foolish in love," said his mum as she walked past him. "Speaking of love, are you seeing anyone now? I still can't understand why you could not follow Lettie to England. She was such a lovely girl."

Scarlett was Eli's high school sweetheart. They had been together for over eight years, before she and her two sisters emigrated to England. She wanted Eli to go with her. She did everything, including sending copies of his résumé to many recruitment agencies. She even managed to secure a few telephone interviews for him. But Eli's heart was not in it. He said he did not want to leave his dying mum and young brother. Scarlett was heartbroken but she understood. She said she would remain hopeful because Eli was the only one she wanted, but the truth was that Eli also needed a break from her. They had been together since their teenage years, and he desperately needed some space. Also deep down, Eli knew that ever since he returned from his secondment in Harare, his mind never let go of that mysterious girl he met in the park.

"Scarlett is in the past now, Ma. Not to guilt you or anything but I felt I was needed here still. I am very happy here. She could have stayed here with me if she really cared for me, for us," responded Eli.

"You had my blessings, son. Nothing would make me more at peace than knowing that you have a good woman, a good companion. The Bible says he who finds a good wife, finds favour with the Lord. But now, I worry."

"It's ok, mum. I have someone; Zahara. She is amazing. You will meet her in time. Oh, I love her, mum," Eli beamed like a teenager.

He stayed the night, and slept in his old bedroom. It always brought past memories, many of them very sad and lonesome. The days of just him and his mum struggling to make ends meet. His mum was an administrator at a doctor's surgery, and she did not earn much. Life was already hard for her raising a boy by herself in a country ruled by apartheid, and where black women were considered third class citizens. He remembered the time they nearly lost the house. He remembered how that month, when the bank wanted the outstanding mortgage payments, his mum slept with a handful of strange men. He knew the neighbours saw those men come in and go. He knew what they thought of his mum. It always tore apart his heart. And then he would often hear of sightings of estranged father in shebeens and downtown bars. Apparently, he had started a new family just outside Soweto. Eli hated him with every part of his being. He often wished he could castrate him and watch him bleed to death. But his mum always said that his father was the best love she ever had. She even dared say that he loved Eli. How could he have loved them and then treated them with such disregard?

He thought about the morning he saw his father when he returned like the Bible's prodigal son. He could not believe that his mum let him stay the night. He had just finished high school and was preparing to go university. He rowed with his father; told him he was not welcome in their house anymore. His father backslapped him, and told him to show him some respect. Eli retaliated; he threw multiple punches and sent him reeling to the ground. He banged his right jaw against the armrest of the lounge chair as he fell. He looked up at Eli, and saw the anger in his eyes. At that moment, he realised that Eli was no longer the same boy he had left years earlier. Like an ageing male lion, his father realised that he really was no longer welcome amongst his old pride anymore. There was a new alpha male that did not like the old guard one bit.

That week Eli's mother tried to make peace between them. She pleaded with Eli to forgive his father, but deep down she knew that her estranged husband had hurt their little boy so much. No matter the intentions, no boy wanted to see their mother whoring to make ends meet. Eli told his mum that it was her choice whether or not to take his father back; but as far as he was concerned, his father was no longer of relevance to his life. With that, Eli left for university in Western Cape.

Three months later when he returned home, he found out that his father only stayed for a week before he disappeared again. But what broke his heart was finding out that his mum was pregnant with his father's child, and that she was keeping it. For that moment, and that moment alone, Eli found some hate for his mum. He hated himself too and his whole existence. He remembered his mum saying, "And I do not want you hearing this from anyone else. I am sorry, son but I am now also positive." When she said that, Eli's heart stopped beating for a moment before he lashed out, "Oh mum, how fucking dumb are you?"

"Hey, watch your mouth. I am still your mother. Have some respect," she said.

"Respect? You work at a doctor's office, and don't you tell people to use protection. This is South Africa for goodness's sake; nearly everyone is fucking positive, and you let that disease-ridden drunk come in here and into your bedroom, and you don't even say no. And you ask me to respect you? Seriously mum?"

He remembered his mum backslapping him too. He felt a panic attack brewing, and he leaned against the wall. For a moment, he did not know how to breathe. He felt cold water flooding every part of his inside. He looked at his mum and could not recognise her. He collapsed to the floor.

He knew he could never stay mad at his mum. He knew deep inside she regretted taking his father back. He therefore knew there was no point probing her about it; and of course, it was now up to him to look after his mum. He had to clean up his father's mess in the best way he could. When Justin was born, and as he held him in his arms, Eli felt intense love and sorrow for his little brother who looked so much like him. He knew this was one bruise on his heart that would never heal.

CHAPTER SIX

6 Eli loved Cape Town since his university days. He knew beautiful parts of the city where the environment was serene. He went there when he wanted quiet moments. He could never find such tranquillity in Pretoria. He loved it. And this time, he loved it even more. It was different; it was not the serenity that he was after. He was riding in a cable car through Table Mountain with the love of his life. He was holding Zahara's hand. His life felt complete. He did not want for anything else. He was not scared of anything else; not even death, as long as he was with her.

"Eli, look at that," Zahara calmly said.

Eli just looked at her and smiled. He felt eyes welling up.

"What's wrong Eli?" asked Zahara.

"Nothing babe, I am just happy. I have never been this happy. I am so happy," he responded.

"Me too, babe. Me too. I know it will never be enough for you, but for what it's worth, I do love you too, Eli. For saving me, and more importantly, for being the best thing that ever happened to me," confided Zahara rubbing her eyes to keep back the tears.

They just held hands for the rest of the ride, occasionally exchanging glances. Eli thought about the fun they had had the previous evening. He remembered their breathlessness as they raced on the beach while the sun set beyond the endless blue horizon. He wished he could freeze such moments. He wanted to hold onto the amazing feeling of endlessness.

CHAPTER SEVEN

---◄◄◄∿∿►►►---

7 They had been together for seven months but Eli still felt mystified by his relationship with Zahara. He loved her with every part of his being, and he had no reason to think that she did not care for him either. But she always seemed to subtly keep him at an arm's length every now and again. Maybe his desire for endlessness made him seem desperate, he thought. She did not even want their relationship labelled.

"Why do we have to put a label on it?" she posed.

"I just need to know. Please for my own sanity. Are you my girlfriend or what? Where are we going?" he retorted.

"I am your best friend, I am your partner, I am your lover. I am everything and anything you want me to be. Just don't… just don't…" she stuttered.

"Just don't what?" asked Eli.

"It's not easy for me, Eli. I don't know. You are the first relationship of some sort I have had. Please just don't… just let it be. What I am to you might not be real to me. Just don't, please. Just love me, Eli," said Zahara as she hugged him.

Eli embraced her back, but a part of his heart sank. Maybe it was just his own insecurity. Maybe it was because she was a model who met so many better men. But Zahara always reassured him that she would never sleep with anyone else. Eli knew from the outset that more commitment from her would be hard, so he told himself he would accept less, if less was all she had to give.

"I know I am away a lot with my work, and sometimes I keep you away. It's not you; it's just that sometimes I need time to myself. But trust me, I will never ever want for another person's touch as long as you are with me. Please believe me."

However, three days before their first anniversary, Eli's heart could not hold it any longer. He wanted in. He wanted more; he realised that he had lied to himself than less would suffice.

"Zahara, please let me in," he caught Zahara unaware as they sat on the sofa having Moroccan food from the local restaurant.

"Oh Eli, what is it? What do you want me to do? I love you, I really do. But have you ever thought that maybe I don't know how to love you the way you want to be loved?" she responded rather sternly.

"What do I want? What do I want?" barked Eli with a whimsical smile on his face. "I just want you to open up to me. For starters, tell me something, tell me anything about your family. You do not want to get close to my family despite my mum welcoming you unreservedly. It is as if you know you are not in this relationship for the long haul. And sometimes when you are away on photo-shoots, you keep me away from you, like I embarrass you in front of your model friends or like you are dating someone from your work. Just tell me, do I have a future with you? Please. What is wrong with the so-called 'labels'? What's wrong with calling a spade, a spade?"

Zahara delayed for a moment. She moved forward and leaned downwards as she pulled her hair. After further hesitation, she said "What I am giving to you is all I have. When there is nothing else to give, how can you ask for more?" She paused again, and stood up and walked to the window and stared into the bright lights of the Pretoria nightscape. "Of all people, I thought you understood the concept of troubled souls, demons and the need for personal space. I have given every part of my body to you. You have kissed every part of me – isn't that enough for a while? When I have more, I will give you more. For now, can you not hang on the fact that you are the only one I love, kiss and cuddle? Please Eli, but I cannot promise you forever; I cannot give you the feeling of endlessness you want."

"Stop speaking in confusing analogies and rhymes. Just be honest with me. Just let me in. Just tell me we have a future together. Give me a little bit more. Who are you? You can't even tell me why you were crying the first time I met you in that park in Harare. You won't tell me why you haven't been back to Zimbabwe since you moved here. It's shade after shade of mystery with you. I have given you everything, yet every day I dread that I am going to lose you. I am on the edge every day, Zahara. I don't want to lose you; just dreading..." he stopped as his voice began to crack.

"Maybe I should go," she said as she walked to the door.

"Ah come on. See? You leave me when I am vulnerable?" queried Eli, but she paid no mind to it.

She would not take his calls the following day. She did not take his calls either on their anniversary three days later. The bouquets of flowers and gift bags he sent her were ineffective. Eli was heartbroken. They were supposed to dine at a Mediterranean restaurant in Sandton. He regretted the evening she walked away. Why could he not have kept his feelings inside? He cursed himself. He wanted to crawl in a dark corner and sob himself to oblivion.

Days passed. A week passed. He knew she was due to travel to Cape Town that week, so he hoped she would at least return his calls before she left. But she did not. Two months passed but nothing. Eli sank into a feeling of helplessness and self-pity.

He did not know what else to do; call, go to her apartment or let her be. He drove past her apartment every evening, but the curtains were always drawn and the lights off. He tried ringing her mobile phone from a public booth but it went to voicemail, and after that, the number became unlisted. Eli was sad. He knew it had been all too good to be true. He got greedy; he should have settled for less.

CHAPTER EIGHT

8 Another two months passed, and Eli was undefinably sad. With each passing day, it was as if a part of him died. His heart was laden with grief. Zahara was gone. Justin was wasting away every day. He could not remember what it felt like when Zahara was there. It seemed like pain was all his heart had known for a long time. He longed for her return. He did not care if she was messing around. He just wanted her back, and he would never ask for more ever again. A fraction of her love was better than no love at all. So many things he missed about her; each and every one of them tormented him like sharp pins in his mind. Why did he get greedy? He hated how love came and went just like that, like it knew exactly what it wanted.

It was just after nine in the morning when Eli got the text message. It was Zahara. She had a new number. It was her finally. He felt hyperventilated. He took a deep breath. She missed him too. She wanted dinner at the *Cozinha Português* restaurant. He walked to the door and continued across the room towards the window. He stood still and stared blankly at the sun shining in the sky. It was like the first time he had ever noticed the sun shining. Everything felt so surreal; he was lost in a sea of incomprehensibility. A few minutes later, he responded to her message.

He had heard of the *Cozinha Português* but he had never been there, neither had he been to that part of Sandton before. The restaurant was full of ambience and style. There was a woman playing an acoustic guitar and singing softly in Portuguese. Eli's eyes wandered around the room searching. Then he saw her, and she was even more beautiful than he remembered. She had cut her hair. She was wearing a short black dress and tomato-red high heels. He walked to her, and hugged her. He was home. His eyes welled up and he cried on her shoulder. He felt like a complete wimp as he cried but he could not help it. She led him outside holding his hand. After he had calmed down, she said, "Eli, I am sorry. All I want to say right now is I still love you too, but for now, let's just have a great evening. Let us dine and dance, and let us lose ourselves in this moment, and not where we have been. Please."

They dined and danced. It was as if they had never been apart. It felt like a new lease of life for Eli's frail heart.

After dinner, Eli drove them back to his flat. As soon as he closed the door, she was all over him. They both needed it. It was crude, it was raw, and it was full of tension. They both enjoyed it. Twice. The first one did not last long, but the second one was perfect. Zahara did things that Eli had never experienced before.

After the sex came the talking. They chatted long into the deepness of the night. She talked. She tried to open up.

"Eli, it has never been about you. It's me with the problems. I know what you want. You want more than just a girlfriend; you want this to go somewhere. You want a wife and a mother for your kids and all that. And you deserve that…"

Eli interjected, "No, that was then. Now, all I want is to be with you. I will gladly settle for less, much less."

"No, no, don't say that. You are lying to yourself. You will always want more, and you do deserve more," she sighed. "The problem is I cannot promise you more than what we have now. I have issues; lots of them. And sometimes it is hard, very hard to wake up in the morning your mind full of demons. It is even harder trying to let someone in; to share anything with anyone," she paused and let Eli's embrace soothe her for a moment. "The reason why I don't go back to Zim is because there is no life for me there. I have no family. I hate my demonic family. It is one big mess, and honestly, I want you to stop before you fall into the massive hole that is me and my past. I do not want to take you down with me. I know this speech sounds rehearsed but it is the truth. I love you, and that is the absolute truth."

"I love you, too," Eli said. "Let me fall with you. I want to fall with you. Nothing matters when I am with you."

"Why should you fall with me? You have done more than enough already. You saved me that afternoon in the park, and you asked for nothing in return. It was the first time, and probably the only time anyone ever did anything for me without expecting anything in return. These past four months

without you were just as hard on me as they were on you…"
Eli tried to interrupt but she hushed him.

"Let me say it. You must understand how hard it has been
for me to get to this point. All I want you to know is that I know
it is unfair on you. I know you said you do not want much
now, but you do not have to compromise for my sake. You will
always want more. Your mum wants grandchildren. You want
a life partner," she paused and cast a glance at Eli and saw how
delicate he had become. He was always so delicate, and she
loved that vulnerability in him. "So, I have come to the decision
that it's okay for you to date someone else, someone you want
to marry. But I selfishly ask that I still remain your friend,
your lover, your whatever you want me to be. Anything you
want me to be. Please. I cannot lose you entirely," she pleaded
with a crackly voice. The delicacy on Eli's face and her own
desperation were a bit much to bear.

"You are not understanding what I am saying. I want to go
with you wherever you are going, be it nowhere or somewhere,"
he said as he gently stroke her hair. "Do you remember that
time when we were in Cape Town, and you asked me to ride
the cable car, and I told you I had a fear of heights?" he asked,
but did not expect Zahara to respond. "Do you know why I
rode the car anyway? It is because when I am with you, I have
no fear whatsoever. The only fear I have is losing you. When
you give me love, I am ready to fall as long as it is with you.
Don't get me wrong, it would be nice to have a house in the
suburbs, to have kids attending private schools and such, but
I would rather plunge into the cold waters of the Antarctica as
long as it is with you. I won't date anyone. I will not again ask
you to give me more than you can because as you put it, when

there is nothing to give, how can we ask for more? Stay with me for as long as you can, for as long as you have to. Whatever you want to do, that is what I will do, as long as I am with you."

He stared into her brown eyes, and saw tears flickering. He embraced her, and squeezed a bit. She squeezed back, and neither of them said another word. They slept in each other's arms. Eli was happy again. His heart could beat again. He was home again and the atmosphere was electric.

The following morning he woke up early to make breakfast; blueberry pancakes with scrambled eggs and fried spicy mushrooms. When he went back to the bedroom, he found Zahara with a sheet wrapped around her, staring at a portrait next to the dressing table.

"That's me, right? I mean this drawing," she asked as she turned to kiss Eli.

He kissed her softly on the lips, and said, "Yes, it is. What gives? The big eyes?" He laughed rather embarrassedly.

"I love it. Who did it?"

"Some guy in Sunnyside. It was when I was going crazy thinking about you."

"And the inscription 'Beautiful Nightmare'?" she laughed.

"That one I did. Actually, it was only last week. I had found some hate for you, you know, just for show," he laughed back, and continued. "I am sorry if it offends you..."

"Actually, I like it. Is that how you see me? A beautiful nightmare? It's melancholic but also sweet and poetic."

Later that day in the afternoon, they went to Eli's mum's house, and they stayed until after dinner. Eli was pleased to see Zahara getting on splendidly with his mum. Justin adored her too. Eli was happy.

"Thank you for a lovely dinner, Ma Zwide," said Zahara as she embraced Eli's mum good-bye.

"The pleasure was mine, dear. Make sure you come again soon, okay? If Eli doesn't want to bring you, come by yourself," she laughed.

"Goodnight Ma," he laughed and kissed her on the cheek. He grabbed Zahara's hand and as they walked towards the car, she looked at him, and said "Here's one more reason why I love you… you have a lovely mum; I love her. And little Justin… anyone ever told you, he looks so much like you?"

"So, it is nothing to do with the fact that I give it to you freakishly good in bed," Eli guffawed. Zahara smiled back and gently smacked him on the back.

Chapter Nine

9 Eli stared at Zahara's long legs and thought about the first time he saw them. They looked silky and smooth under her translucent nightdress. She knew he was looking, and she let him. Underneath her skin, her whole body was filled with warmth. For the first time in her life, she was in love. She was floating; felt as light as a feather. She cast a glance at him. She had told him that she had a lot of skeletons in her closet, but she hoped he would never be able to see through to the imperfections of her soul. She knew she had to fight the memories of ghosts past. Her heart was in a good place, and nothing ought to interrupt the feelings that Eli had stirred in her.

"Say sweetie, is it okay if I move some of my stuff here?" she asked as she continued applying moisturiser to her legs.

"Of course, you can. I cannot believe you are even asking me that. You know very well that when we are apart, I am a desperate for you, and when you are here, I forget how fragile the world is," he responded. He knew a simple 'yes' or 'no' would have sufficed but he loved being elaborate.

"I know, but are you sure your mum will be okay with us living in sin?" she asked with a whimsical smile.

"I would take happiness any day over fear of sin," remarked Eli and laughed. "I am soaked in your love!"

"That's a good thing, I guess?" she asked.

"You bet your sweet ass it is. It's the best thing that's ever happened to me, and I still can't get enough," responded Eli. If he had his way, this feeling would never end. But he had learnt his lesson; he would never again ask for more than she had to give. Whether an hour or a decade, genuine or pretend, Eli had told himself he would gladly accept what she had to give.

"Great," she said as she jumped on to the bed and next to him. "I do love you, you know that? I am sorry for walking out on you before. But believe me when I say that I love this place; this moment. You make my heart sing."

"Love you too," he said as his left hand stroked her legs. "The important thing is we are back together, and these past three months have been the best days of my life."

"Right back at you. Now come on, make me moan," she said as she nibbled on his ear.

"When are you off to Durban for that Christmas shoot?" he asked as he turned to kiss her.

"A week from tomorrow," she whispered. "Come on, show me how you do that trick that makes me scream with ecstasy."

Her love was his asylum, and he was overjoyed to have her firmly back; the mental craziness was gone and the emotional bruises were healing.

Chapter Ten

10 Eli hated evenings when Zahara was away. The only upside was that it had given him time to do his Christmas shopping, he thought as he sat down to eat the pizza he had picked up on his way from work. He hated cooking on Fridays.

He looked at the clock, and it had just gone past seven. He realised he had to call Zahara before she went to her evening reception, which she said was scheduled for 8pm.

She did not pick up. He ate another slice before trying again. Again she did not answer. He thought nothing of it, and rationalised that maybe she went early. He finished his dinner, and watched the Friday night movie on TV before gently drifting into sleep on the couch.

He checked his phone when he woke up and realised he was still on the couch. It was just before two o'clock. He switched off the TV and staggered towards the bathroom. As he brushed his teeth, it occurred to him that he had rung Zahara earlier. He checked his phone; there were no text messages or missed calls. He shuddered with jealousy. The thought of Zahara sleeping in someone else's arms cut through his heart. His hands shook. He dialled her number without any thought. There was an answer, finally. But it was not Zahara. But it was a woman's voice.

"Hello, Zee's phone," she said.

"Hello?" asked Eli rather befuddled.

"Yes, hello, it's Zahara's phone, who is it?" she responded rather agitated.

"Can I speak with Zahara, please? It's her, um, her friend from Pretoria," he said. He had not prepared for that.

"Oh, I am sorry, Zahara is in... sorry, who are you again? Your number just showed up as 'E'," she said with apprehension in her voice.

"Is everything alright? My name is Eli, and I am her boyfriend. Where is she?" he said hurriedly.

"She collapsed earlier, so we are in hospital in Durban."

"Is she alright? I am on my way," he said loudly as he breathed hard. "Can you keep her phone for longer? I will ring you from my car. I am on my way."

It took Eli just under four hours to drive approximately 300 miles to Durban.

"Hi, you must be Eli," said the mixed race girl, a 'Cape-coloured' to be specific. She had big front two white teeth. Her lips were big too, especially the upper one. She was very tall; almost a foot taller than Eli. "I'm Lenore or Len for short; I work with Zee."

"Hi Len," he said as he offered his hand. "I have heard of you. Have you heard anything from the doctors since we last spoke?"

"They said they wanted next of kin. So, we had to ring our boss to see who Zee has listed as the emergency contact, and it turns out it is you."

"So, where do I go?" He was jittery and sweating profusely. "Well Len what really happened?"

"Well, it started just when we got here a week ago. Initially, it was just nausea, and she vomited a couple of times, and we both thought maybe she was pregnant. She took a pregnancy test and it was negative. Then yesterday morning she complained of fatigue and shortness of breath, but come on, we are models. Our job is fucking demanding that's why everyone pretty much smokes. And then when we were going to the evening reception yesterday, she complained about flank pain and dizziness. So, we asked the cab driver to take us here, and as we were getting out of the cab, she collapsed. And I have been here since, and haven't seen her, so really don't know what it is going on. They have been stalling me, saying that she is unwell and they need next of kin."

They walked over to reception, and Len leaned over and said to the gentleman sat behind the desk, "Eh brother, the next of kin is here for my friend in 102."

Moments later, an Indian woman walked towards them and motioned Eli. She looked at Lenore hesitantly, but Eli said, "It's ok, she is a close family friend."

"Hello. I am Doctor Gurkhaat," she said as she sat next to Eli. "It appears Zahara's kidneys have both failed. We have given her some sedation drugs, and hooked her onto a dialysis machine but she needs a new kidney very soon." Eli was speechless. The doctor placed her hand on Eli's shoulder, and continued, "Do not worry, she is in safe hands here; we will do our best. We will be taking her out of sedation in a few hours' time, and you can see her then."

Lenore started crying.

After a moment of eerie silence, Eli finally asked "Is there anything I can do?"

"Well, other than getting her a new kidney, no, there is nothing anyone can do. We have registered an urgent request for a donor kidney but her blood type is AB, which is very rare in black people..."

"So, she can't get a kidney from a white donor because of her rare blood type?" Len interjected.

"No, no, no," protested the doctor. "I am just trying to give you the clear picture of the challenge that we have."

"I have the same blood type as her. We once donated blood together, and we were told we had the same blood type. Does that mean I am a match?" Eli said. He did not wait for the doctor to respond, "I want to be her donor."

"Of course, you can, but we would have to undertake some tests first," she said cautiously. "We can do that easily, but don't you want to talk to her first? She should be up in another three hours or so," she added as she looked at her watch.

Eli cast a quick glance at Lenore, who had stopped crying and was visibly surprised, and said "No. What difference does it make? She needs a kidney, I have one, and I want to give it to her. I would rather do it now."

"I do not mean to disrespect your wish, sir, but donating a kidney should not be an impulsive decision, which is why we also undertake psychiatric tests to check that you also have good mental health. Life with one kidney is very challenging, and there is always a risk of complications during the operation. Also there is no guarantee that her system will accept the donated kidney. This is why we ask live donors to take time to consider the decision to donate organs," responded the doctor calmly. She looked at Lenore as if to seek vindication or support. Lenore said nothing back. She had not seen that coming. She had never anticipated anyone making the kind of sacrifice Eli was about to make.

But Eli would not be moved, and a few tests later, they confirmed he was a match.

As they wheeled him into the Operating Room, he tried not to think about the risks. He thought only about seeing Zahara again. He knew it was a rash decision. How would his boss take the news that he was going to be off work for three months? What would his mum say? He tried not to think about it. He just thought of Zahara; the disturbed soul that he thought only he understood. He longed to feel her magic again.

Lenore trotted after them and said, "Eli, in case, you know something happens, is there anything you want to tell her?"

"Thanks Len, but she already knows," he responded softly.

CHAPTER ELEVEN

11 Daylight awakened him. He had slept for over twelve hours. He opened his eyes and speculated for a moment about where he was. The sound of beeping machines to his left jogged his memory. He shifted slightly and turned to face his right. There was a hand clasping his. She was sleeping like an angel on the bed next to his. He watched her sleep, and thought about how much he had missed her. He was slightly startled when she opened her eyes without warning, and forced a weary smile.

"How could you?" she asked with disappointment in her voice and as her eyes welled up.

Eli did not say anything back. He just squeezed her hand, and shifted his eyes to stare blankly at the ceiling.

"You had some complications, they said they nearly lost you," she continued. He squeezed her hand a bit tighter, and she squeezed back. "Your mum is on her way down."

The mention of his mum jolted his whole body. He stared at the ceiling for longer. He knew what exactly what she was going to say. He felt awful for making her travel, and leaving Justin, probably with the neighbours. For a moment, he regretted his decision. His mind scrambled for happy thoughts. He then turned to Zahara and said, "There are things I cannot explain with words but when I am with you the world stops for me. No one, nothing will ever interrupt those feelings. I would die a thousand times if it means I get another night to spend with you." Still, he could see the strong look of hurt and disappointment that was going to be on his mum's face.

Zahara said nothing back. She just let tears roll down her cheeks.

CHAPTER TWELVE

―⸻⸻―

12 Life after the operation was hard for Eli as reality bit. The post-operation pain was more than he had envisaged. Even after three months, he did not feel wholly well, but he had to go back to work especially since Zahara was told to stay put for at least six months. Zahara did not mind. In her mind, she felt it was the right thing to do; spend more time with the man who had saved her twice.

Eli's mum was deeply hurt with the choice her son had made. She had affection for Zahara but still she was indignant about Eli's decision. "How could you be so idiotic to just throw your life away like that? Now I have two unwell sons," she said at the hospital as she sobbed.

Eli hated seeing her cry, but he calmly explained, "I love her, ma. Was I supposed to un-love her because her kidneys had stopped functioning? I know it's not the best decision I have ever made but haven't we all done stupid things in the name of love?"

She knew he was right. She saw the love in his eyes, and so she held her hurt and anger inside. She paused for a long time and then calmly said, "I understand the sacrifice you made, Eli. I know first-hand the things that love can make you do, but those things can live to become the things you regret the most."

Once they were back in Pretoria, she visited Eli's apartment many times, to check on Eli and Zahara. She resented that Zahara now lived there. She was always there. Ma Zwide longed for quiet moments with her son, just like it was when his father left. She did, however, find him by himself one Saturday morning.

"Ma, you don't have to keep coming and checking on me. I am fine. My kidney is fine. The doctors gave me the all-clear, that is why I am back at work," explained Eli.

"Argh," she said and forced a wry smile, "Can't a mother just visit her son without having to justify it?"

"It's okay, ma, really," responded Eli. "Thanks for the food, the cleaning and such. We really appreciate it and Zahara really loves your food."

"You know we never talked about you and her living together. I did not raise you that way..." she protested but Eli interrupted.

"Ma, please let's not go there. My sinful choices are mine to live with. All that should matter to you is whether or not I am happy, and I will tell you now, I am happy. And I would rather live a short and sinful but happy life than a long miserable one."

"You have always been as stubborn as a donkey!" she said rather miffed. "Take it from me happiness in sinful ways will not last, but since you are so adamant, then it is not my place. Where is Zahara anyway because there is something I need to talk to you about in confidence?"

"She has an appointment for another dose of immunosuppressants," he explained.

"Ok," she said and paused for a moment. She clasped her hands and looked at Eli. "I do not think Justin has much time, Eli. The pain is now getting worse, and I cannot stand watching him waste away anymore."

"I know, ma but he is valiant that boy; braver than I will ever be," remarked Eli.

"I can get some morphine for him from our surgery," she said. Eli looked baffled. He stared at his mum, and could tell that the statement was incomplete. "I want to put him out of his anguish. It is time for my special little boy to rest, um, and sleep with the angels," she said with misty eyes.

Eli finally understood. He did not respond. He let it stew in his mind. About ten minutes later, he softly uttered, "When?"

"I don't know. Soon. Once we have both said our good-byes," she responded.

Five weeks later, Justin died as he slept. Eli had known about it. He had gone through it in his mind a million times, but when it eventually happened, Eli realised that one could never plan for death of a loved one. He grieved for his little brother. For him, it was another reminder of the many iniquities of his estranged father. He hated him some more. He did not come to the funeral; but perhaps no one told him. Besides, Eli would not have wanted him there anyway.

Justin lied so peacefully in the mahogany casket. Everything he wore had a shade of blue; his favourite colour. Eli paused and stared at his little brother's lifeless body, and the pain struck him violently. Their brotherly bond had always been very strong. He felt regretful how Justin's life had turned out, but perhaps, this life was not for him. His little brother who thought Eli was Superman; the little boy everyone said was as sweet as the Psalms. As the men from the funeral home shovelled back the earth, other mourners stood back to avoid the rising dust. Eli stood there oblivious to his surroundings. Tears flowed down his cheeks and mingled with the dust. Zahara moved forward and clasped Eli's arm. She saw how exposed and lost he was, and she wept with him; her heart in one accord with his.

CHAPTER THIRTEEN

13 It was Eli's twenty-seventh birthday. As he drove back from work, he expected another surprise from Zahara. She loved surprises on special occasions. She had asked him to scuttle back home immediately after work. Eli thought they would probably go out for dinner, followed by a night of passionate romance; well, great sex, even though he wondered how else it could get better. Zahara was not a great cook. Besides, they had hardly been out since the kidney transplant operation. He felt a tingle of excitement inside as he opened the door.

Zahara stood in the hallway wearing white silk short length gown which showed her long legs. It took Eli by surprise. He felt blood rushing through his body. She stood there smiling.

"Hey babe," she said as she kissed him on the lips. Eli back-heeled the door and slammed it shut.

"Hey," that's all he could say.

"Happy birthday, darling. I have a special evening planned for my special boy," she said as she led him into their open-plan kitchen and dining room. The whole apartment was filled with soft aria music; her favourite music which he had also grown to like.

The table was already set; just plates, glasses and cutlery. There were bowls on the cooker, and some on the kitchen counter. Eli was impressed that she had cooked a special dinner for him. He knew how much she hated cooking.

"How did you do all this?" he asked excitedly.

"Well, a few recipes from the newspaper cut-outs. Of course, I had to redo a couple of the dishes," she laughed.

She opened the pots and said, "In here, creamy garlic mushrooms; red kidney bean rice in that one. These two have Scottish salmon with white wine and prawn cream sauce or something. For dessert, I have made creamy lemon ice cream… not so sure about that one. I hope you will like it, anyway." She laughed and paused. "If not, you can always have this for dessert instead," she said as she stepped back and opened the gown. Eli's whole body jerked forward when he saw her lush and firm breasts. She wore nothing underneath the gown except laced black pants. She stood with legs slightly parted. She closed the gown, and teased, "I am up here, babe."

Eli felt warm in his heart. As the *Nessun dorma* high notes filled the apartment, tenderness gushed down his whole body.

"It translates *'and my kiss will dissolve the silence that makes you mine',*" Zahara explained, before holding his cheeks and whispering, "And this means you are the only boy I have ever loved." She kissed him. He embraced her tightly as he kissed her back and murmured, "I love you too, Zahara. I really do. I love you sweetheart more than anyone else has ever loved or will ever love. Thank you for this, for everything and the food looks great."

"We are not eating yet though," she said as she pulled his hand. "First, we make passionate love. I don't want you humping me on a full stomach." She giggled as she walked into the bedroom with Eli closely behind. He quickly stripped to his boxers and sat on the bed. He watched her tease him as she mouthed the opera song pretending to be on stage. She leaned forwards and kissed him passionately, and then she moved back, and continued to lip sync to the aria vocals. Eli looked at her breasts, and imagined how hard her nipples were. She moved forward again, and let him feel them. He gasped as he touched them. She climbed onto the bed. As the music bellowed, she continued to tease. She knelt next to him and kissed his nipples. She tried to stand up again. But Eli felt an implosion inside him, and he could not hold back. He grabbed her, and laid on her the bed as he ripped apart her knickers.

It was without doubt Eli's greatest day; he could not be happier. He had no fear of death at that moment; he was finally content with his life. Every passing moment was perfect. He had never felt so high in his life. He thought about the time when he was seven, and his mum bought him a brand new bike, and he had been the only kid on their block to have it. That was a special moment, but this felt a million times better. He prayed the moment would never turn into a memory of the past.

CHAPTER FOURTEEN

—◦◦◦◦◦—

14 It was a great year for Eli made up of so many tiny perfect moments. Life with Zahara was finally beyond perfection; she was finally his and his alone. Every night in bed with her felt like sailing among the stars; he felt closer to the moon, the heavens, everything. Life was beyond perfection; the only thing missing was his little brother. He often wished someone could freeze time so that he could forever bask in the best moments of his life. He knew it would not last; that was always his luck. Even his mum was doing better than he thought she would be doing, albeit all alone without Justin's infectious laugh. He felt sad for her. He missed him too. Greatly. As they drove back from an evening with her, Eli thought about how devastated he would be if Zahara was ever to leave him again.

"Marry me, Zahara," said Eli as soon as they entered the apartment.

"Come on babe, we have talked about this before," responded Zahara.

"Well, I will wear you down one day," laughed Eli trying to hide his hurt.

"You know that I would if I could. Why do you care so much about that? You have me, all of me and you know that. Hell or high water, I am all yours forever. I just don't want you to worry your life away wishing for the perfect world instead of enjoying what we have. Don't make me feel inadequate, please Eli," she said earnestly. "Why does it matter to you whether we are married or not? You said you do not care much for social conformities."

"I don't know. I want it all, I guess or maybe anything to give me some added security that you will not leave me again," he responded.

"I love you, Eli. I will be with you till death do us part, ok. My heart is yours and yours alone, and so is my wedding ring finger, ok. Let's enjoy our moments nonchalantly, like we were birds perched on the roof. This past year has been perfect; it is what I would want heaven to be like. Ever since I met, you have been my protector, and through the storms, you have stood strong for me. That's more than I ever asked for or imagined. I love you so."

"Ok, my darling, I did not mean it that way," said Eli. "I just want to have you with me, inside me, all over me, if you know what I mean."

"I know babe," she said as she stroked his arm. "I will never leave you, I promise."

"Phew. If you leave me, I will kill you, and then I will commit suicide just so I can kill you again," he laughed uncomfortably before adding, "I am kidding, of course."

Zahara kissed him on the cheek as she stood up. She gazed at him and smirked. She debated in her head when it would be the right time to tell him that her kidney was failing. Her body was rejecting the donor kidney; Eli's kidney. The immuno-suppressants were not working. She had kept all that from Eli.

"Hey," said Eli calmly as he stood up and moved next to her. He put his arms around her neck, and said "You know I was joking about the killing you thing? You know me; the only thing I can kill are roaches."

She grinned and nodded.

Eli continued, "I am sorry, sweetheart. I do not mean to hound you about this. It's my own insecurity. I feel reborn; I feel super-alive when I am with you. Been through many shitty times, you know with my dad leaving, Justin dying, my mom being sick and so on, but when I am with you, all that hurt has no room in my heart. Somehow your love sets it all free."

She looked at him and saw the glow of love in his eyes that she had being accustomed to. She felt empathetic. She felt soaked and overwhelmed by his warm affection and sincerity. No man had ever loved her like that. She felt her eyes well up and she could not control it. She whimpered.

"What is it, Zahara?" asked Eli sounding rather mystified. She did not say a word. She sat on the couch, and sobbed hysterically.

"Zahara, you are scaring me? What's the matter?" Eli asked again as he sat next to her, and put his arm around her. She cried for a long five minutes. Eli just sat next to her silently, patting her back. He then went out of the room and brought back tissue paper and a glass of water.

"Thank you," Zahara finally said as she wiped her eyes and nose. "I love you, Eli. I really do. By far, you are the best thing that ever happened to me."

"I love you, too. You know that," said Eli.

"I know," she said and paused. "My kidney has failed again."

"What do you mean?" blurted Eli with obvious distress in his voice. "You look okay. Are you in pain? Who said the kidney has failed?"

"I have been on haemodialysis for the past three weeks. I go to the hospital every other day now. The kidney has not actually failed as yet, but it's a matter of time. I am sorry I didn't tell you before. Everything was just perfect."

"Ok," he said trying to be calm. "Am sure we can get another one." He clasped his hands together and took a deep breath.

"I know we should be positive, Eli, but there is a chance that this could be it," she said.

"Don't talk like that," he rebuked her softly. "I read somewhere that people can live on dialysis for years. We can save money for a dialysis machine at home."

She looked at him, and saw how shaken he was. He could not take any more bad news. The immunosuppressants were giving her lymphoma which was now attacking her liver. The consultant had told her that it was imperative that she started chemotherapy straightaway, in the hope that she would get another liver donation soon. He had told her that the odds were against her. Without chemo, she had three or maybe four months.

"It's okay, my darling. You will be fine," Eli tried to reassure her. "We deserve spending a long time together. Someone in our families is due this – staying in love and growing old. We will grow old together. You are going to be fine."

"Eli, the consultant also said my liver is failing because of the drugs I have been taking to help my kidney. I know you tried. We tried, but it does not look good at all." She took his hand and stroked it. Eli stood up and paced around the room, and it broke her heart, so she lied "He said the odds are good if I start chemotherapy right away."

"Let us move to England," he said a few seconds later. "There is better treatment there. I know a few people there."

"You think your ex-girlfriend will want to help me? It's okay really, Eli. We will stay here and fight it together, but more importantly, let's just enjoy each and every moment, you know, make the best of whatever time we have together."

"See, that's not good mentality there," pouted Eli. "You are talking like you have already made your peace with not being here. Let's go to England. I had some job offers a few years back; I can try again. Please."

"Eli, do you ever wonder if this is just destiny catching up with me?" she asked. "You know that movie where some people missed a flight which then crashed, and then death hunted them down one by one? Maybe this is me. Twice you have saved me, and I owe you my life for that, but maybe, my number has been up for a long time, and you know you cannot continue to mess up destiny's plans. Or it could be like that 'butterfly effect' thing or whatever."

"Zahara, what has gotten into you? You are a fighter. We will fight this, ok?" he said as he returned to the couch and sat next to her.

"I know, and I know you mean well," she responded calmly. "Maybe I am just tired of running. Maybe I am tired of fighting. Maybe I have given it all I have to give. Maybe I want to leave on a high, you know, and this is the happiest I have ever been. I am just being honest."

Eli looked at her. He felt angry inside. Maybe he was being selfish but why was she doing that to him. He loved her. She was his life.

"I will try to fight, babe," she said as if she had sensed the rage brewing inside him. "I will try, but for what it's worth, you gave me the best days of my life; and for that I will love you forever." She leaned on his shoulder. She felt tears rolling down her left eye. They sat there silently for twenty minutes. Eli finally broke the silence. "If you really want to go, can I go with you?" he asked.

Zahara was shocked by the question. She did not know how to respond. She knew what he meant but still asked, "What do you mean?"

"I mean, you know. I read about people in America or Europe who do these suicide pacts, and they just die together," he explained.

"And why would you want to do such a stupid thing?" blurted out Zahara visibly unhappy with the suggestion.

"Come on now, do not be such a hypocrite," argued Eli. "It's ok for you to want to die but not ok for me to want to die with you?"

"It's different. I am fucking terminally ill and dying anyway, and you are not. Why would you want to do that?" she asked again.

"Well, my mum always says that the world will end someday soon. So, I figure, I would rather end my world with you and on a high like you said earlier."

Zahara had no response. Eli hesitated for a moment before continuing, "Look my sweet darling, I will never know why fate brought us together, and I still do not understand why you continue to choose me. I do not even know much about your past, your family or where you come from, but it does not matter; because as long you are here with me, I do not need to know. You are all that matters. So, wherever you go, I want to be there by your side. I will follow you to hell if that is what it will take for us to spend eternity together. So, when your lights go out, let me go with you."

"Eli, I know you mean well, but you cannot do that," she finally responded. "Your number is not up, and you cannot die on my account. You have so much life to live."

"I don't want any life if it's not with you," he said. "Think about it; what do I have to live for? My little brother is long gone. My mom is terminally ill, and my father is a dick. What do I have to live for?"

"I will try to fight it, Eli. I will," she tried to reassure him, "but promise me something; whatever happens, you will NOT do anything silly because if you do, I will never forgive you. Even in the afterlife."

"Ok," he responded and paused before elaborating, "Ok, only if you are promising to fight." He took her hand and they walked to the bedroom.

Chapter Fifteen

⟞⟋⟍⟋⟍⟞

15 She had the first dose of chemotherapy, and she hated it. It made her sick and nauseated. She vomited most of the time, and she needed the toilet a lot more than usual. She hated that it made her a burden to Eli. He had to look after her. She knew that it would only be a matter of time before Eli would start to see her as a sick girlfriend rather than just girlfriend. She did not want that. It was then she decided that she was not going to fight it. She was going to enjoy the few remaining moments with the only boy she had ever loved. She did not want Eli's last memories of her to be of her in a bedridden state.

It was exactly seven weeks after the talk with Eli. She waited until he was sound asleep before creeping out of bed. All her affairs were in order. Fate was on her side; even her old flat was sold within two weeks of listing. Destiny was calling; everything was falling into place, and everything would go to Eli and no one else. She owed him a lot more than that.

As she downed the Valium tablets, she felt cold heaviness in her heart; broken-hearted that she was doing that to Eli but she figured that was the best way. Her number was up, and Eli had given her all there was to give; there was nothing left.

She went back to bed, and put her arms around Eli. She closed her eyes and slowly drifted into a horizon of thoughts. She felt a cold flush through her body but it did not bother her. Her mind was in a whirl spin. Chronic chattering. She saw the vision of her parents lying in the pool of their own blood. She saw her old brother mouthing "I am sorry, sis", as he dropped a butcher's knife from his left hand. She felt uplifted as that thought disappeared from her mind. She caught glimpses of the many businessmen, politicians and the like she had bedded in Harare in exchange for financial favours and modelling contracts. She saw their potbellies, and unshaven and unkempt privates, and she wanted to puke. Nonetheless, as soon as the visions came, they vanished; and in no matter all the bad thoughts seemed no more than mirages.

Her mind was blank and peaceful. All that remained were thoughts of Eli. His pretty smile when he walked up to her in that park in Harare. The sincerity cast in his eyes, and the earnest tone that shrouded his voice. The demons were finally gone from her mind. All that remained was her precious Eli. He had been like a breeze in the middle of a summer's eve. The happy moments played in her mind like a sweet tune; her very last song. Her only regrets were the words she did not say to Eli. She wished she had let him into her past. All the things she could have shared but could not; scared of what he would have thought of her. She had locked it all in her head, because she felt like she was the only safe person she could tell it to but now she wished she had trusted Eli with her past. And then it hit her;

she did not want to die. He was right; they deserved eternity together. She wanted Eli forever. She wished she had married him; given him all that he had longed for but sometimes even when she was at her happiest, there was nothing more she wanted than to be alone; she never understood why.

She tried to open her eyes but they had become too heavy. She tried to speak. She muttered "Eli... Eli, sweetie, wake up. Help me..." She felt him shifting as he changed sides. She felt his arm around her, enveloping her as his warmth flowed through her body. She wished she could move her arm too and touch him, but she felt not in control of her limbs. She felt cold water enveloping her whole body. Cold, cold water. Darkness began to unfold around her as her eyes began to close. She tried to fight it but she felt exhausted. Eventually, she closed her eyes and drew her last breath. The penance was paid, and her spirit was finally liberated.

Her life had been a fight right to the finish. A battle against demons. The past never left. It was always there lurking with murkiness, until it had trapped her and caged her. She experienced hurt at a young age, and had yearned for solace for a very long time. Then she met Eli. Sweet, beautiful Eli; but it was too late; there was so much wrongdoing in her past, and the penance finally came at a dear price.

Chapter Sixteen

16 Daylight and the sound of a car horn woke him up. It was unlike him to oversleep. Even on Saturdays, Eli was often up by seven. He got out of bed and went to the bathroom. When he got back and he opened the blinds, and said "Babe, wake up. We need to get ready for your treatment. I was hoping we would pass through my mum's on our way. So, rise and shine, my beautiful darling."

When she did not respond, he pulled the duvet. She hated it but it always worked, especially when they were stretched for time. Not this time; she did not move. He moved towards her head, and as he did, he saw a note on the bedside table. He opened it. It read "I am sorry, babe. I am forever indebted to your sweet heart. I am really sorry. Love you forever and always."

He jumped on to the bed, and shook her. "Zahara, come on wake up. Please wake up," he yelled. Her body was cold. Her eyes were closed. She looked peaceful. There was a trace of a smile on her mouth. She did not look dead.

Eli grabbed the phone and dialled for emergency services. He went back to her, and tried chest compressions. He tried until the paramedics got there. They found him muttering, "Zahara, please don't go. Don't go, please, I am begging. Stay with me, babe please." Even as the paramedics attended to her, Eli sat on the floor rocking himself; still mumbling under his breath and with tears running down his eyes, "You are the only thing I need to get by. Just stay Zahara. Please God, do not take her yet."

"I am sorry sir but she is gone," said one of the paramedics. "I am really sorry, sir, but could you please tell us which morgue we should take her body to?"

Eli just shook his head. He did not respond. He stared at her lifeless face, so pretty and serene. Why did he go to sleep last night? He thought about those mornings he had woken early just so he could stare at her, and often wondered what was on her mind. Not this morning; why did he oversleep? He tried to visualise her dying, closing her eyes and succumbing to the deep sleep.

He desperately longed for her. Perhaps, it was his fault, asking her to give so much so soon. Now he felt lost without her; what was life without her? He felt a thorn in his heart, but it gave no pain. His whole body was numb with pain. Eli opened his mouth as he tried to speak. No words came out. He felt his head spinning on a dizzy edge. He felt breath being forced from his lungs. He tried to move but he felt paralysed. "Come back to me," he screamed in his head. He tried to suck in air but could not. He collapsed to the floor.

CHAPTER SEVENTEEN

17 Eli was devastated. He looked out the window and stared at the bright orange sun smiling from a far, and he hated it. The world should have stopped when Zahara died. He shut his eyes to the sunshine and went to sleep in the daytime.

When he finally woke up, he felt like he had been asleep for days. He could not bear the thought of walking past the familiar places he had walked with the woman he loved endlessly. She was gone, and all he could hear were people asking him how he was doing. How did they think he was doing? He was sick and tired of their facile comments asking him to look to God for solace and comment, and asking him to be strong like a man; filling his sorrow with borrowed meaningless words. They would never understand the love he had for her. They did not understand how overwhelmed he was by grief. Their world was different to his, and they could never understand the hurt that was in his desolate and absent heart; he was drowning in a raging sea of grief and depression. Even with mourners surrounding him, he found himself alone, lost and longing for death. Not even the sweet Robin, they had nicknamed Rosetta, singing from the window sill could comfort him. He wanted to die; desperately.

His mind was hazy and his thoughts were distorted. He felt at war; fighting his mind and heart from accepting the reality of his love long gone. So, he found solace in bottles of cheap wine, and overindulged in bad whiskey that he kept by his bedside. He played tangle with her invisible hair, muttering words to the pillow that she used. He wished he had written down every word she had said to him. He could not remember anymore how it felt to be happy. He could feel his body shedding weight, and he did not care.

He felt psychotic. There were voices in his head; but there was one familiar one – he had heard it before. It told him to look back. How could he have not foreseen this? Their relationship appeared doomed from the start. They met with a goodbye hug on that sunny afternoon in Harare. He should have known that a love like that would never last. He was destined to be miserable and in endless pain just like his mum. That was their family's curse! Lucky Justin, he thought, he died young and innocent.

Oh little Justin, ever so strong and resilient. Brave until the end when their mother ended his pain. He had to be brave too; for Zahara. She was all Eli had. No family, just Eli. He lied still on the bed, and watched a black spider crawl across unshaven face. He watched it dance before it scurried away. He thought about how it felt to have no care in the world; he envied the spider.

Eli stood at the altar. He wiped tears from his eyes and cleared his throat before reading the tribute he had prepared.

I remember it well,
The first time that I saw your face,
The tears in your eyes
But your beauty still dazzled my mind
And time stopped moving
I remember it well
The pounding of my heart
As I searched for words to say
To the most beautiful girl I had ever seen
Your pretty mouth as you opened it to speak
And I felt the hurt in your voice
From that moment, all I ever wanted was to take the hurt away

I remember it well
The smile on your face when you came looking for me,
I floated.
But now you are gone
Taken away by the angel of death
Your story is nothing more than what is left in my heart
But these old streets are cold
And I am lost without you
And I wonder if the best days of my life are now past me
Or whether you will realign the stars above my head
So that I will forever travel with you

It was a broken night
When you quietly flew above the clouds without me

You knew how much I always loved flying with you
So as each day goes and night falls,
I relive the torment of your departure
Still I hope that all was well with your flight
And that as you journeyed into outer space,
The angels led the way
And that the prayers I made kept you safe
And took you home to your other dearly departed
I hope you will wait for me in a place that warm and safe
Because I still have so much more to give you and so much
to tell you
Promise me you will find your way back to me where you
belong
For when we are together, all our hurts end
For that reason and more, nothing will ever remove the
beautiful stain of your love from my heart
So sleep in heavenly peace, my beautiful
Sleep in peace Zahara and wait for me
My beautiful nightmare, forever mine

"And to end," he paused and wiped tears and snort from his face. "To end, I will read a directly translated verse from what was her favourite aria "Dido's lament":

When I am laid, am laid in earth;
May my wrongs create no trouble…
No trouble in thy breast;
Remember me, remember me, but forget my fate.
Remember me, but forget my fate.

I will remember you forever. I will remember you, Zahara. I will forever remember you my beautiful nightmare. In a few years' time, they might forget you, or forget the love you shared with me but I will always remember you, and I will come find you wherever you are. I will love you forever."

As the soothing sound of "Ave Maria" filled the church, mourners shook Eli's hand before walking past Zahara's body as it lay in state.

Then a man with a ragged face and approximately his age approached him, and shook his hand too. He leaned over and whispered, "I'm Mori. I am Zahara's brother." He paused as if waiting for Eli to respond. "She rang me a two weeks or so ago. I only got here yesterday, and… Thank you for taking care of my little sister. I doubt she told you much about me, but when we last spoke, she told me about you. The service is beautiful, thank you." Eli did not know what to say. He just squeezed Mori's hand as he looked into his eyes and saw some resemblance. He was pleased to have met a relative of Zahara.

"Thank you for coming Mori," Eli finally whispered back. "I hope you can stay, and we can have a chat."

Mori nodded, and then walked to the casket. There she lay, his beautiful little sister. So peaceful, so serene. She had not changed much since the last time he saw her five years earlier. It took him to a time when they were young, and used to share a bedroom. He stared at her for a while longer, and thought how much they used to talk about crossing the sea to a different world; a world they made up each night as they chatted before drifting to sleep.

He felt annoyed that other people were just passing by, and not stopping to feel the magic of his beautiful sweet sister as she lay there. They did not know her as much as he did. They did not understand her. No one ever did understand her beautiful and complicated mind. He leaned over to kiss her forehead, and whispered "This life was never for you, little sis. I hope you have found your peace at last." He was relieved for her, but felt strange sadness. He felt cold; cold from nothing at all as it dawned that she was never coming back. It struck him violently, and his body shook as emotions filled him. He wept loudly as he knelt next to casket. Even at their worst of times, she was the best friend he had ever had. He bawled, oblivious to the other mourners. He stood up, and walked up to Eli. "I am really sorry for your loss, Eli," he said with a crackle in his voice. "I am sorry I cannot stay. I am sorry." He stepped down from the platform, and made for the exit as onlookers continued to stare.

After the service, Lenore walked up to Eli and hugged him tenderly, and softly remarked "You did well, Eli. She would be very proud of you."

"Thank you," he said with hurt in his voice, as he fought back the tears.

"Oh, this is Izzie and Nina," she said as she introduced two girls who stood either side of her. "We are... we were in the same agency with Zee."

"I am so sorry," said Nina as she rubbed Eli's shoulder. "If you need anything, anything at all... Maybe you could come to my house for dinner or call me for a chat..."

Lenore cut her off, "Nina, shut it." She then said softly, "Zee's body is still there, and you are already hitting on her boyfriend?"

"Well, I am just trying to be nice," responded Nina.

"Oh give me a break," said Lenore with indignation in her voice. "Izzie, take her away please."

As Nina and Izzie walked away, Nina looked back at Eli, and mouthed "I will call you." She turned to Izzie and said, "That bitch just want him for herself. Zee this, Zee that, my ass."

"Come on Nina, you were too in his face," said Izzie.

"Ah, don't give me that. Life is for the living. Is it wrong to offer him comfort in his time of need?" she said remorselessly.

"Comfort?" posed Izzie sarcastically. "You just want to fuck his brains out, don't you?"

"Wouldn't you? He is gorgeous and sensitive. He almost makes me want to settle down," said Nina as they exited the chapel.

"I am sorry about that, Eli," said Lenore. "She is a cut-throat bitch that one. I guess it comes with the territory; modelling business is kind of full selfish people, looking out for no one but themselves; vultures, in fact. Of course, Zee was different." She paused expecting Eli to say something, but he just stared across. "So, what will you do with the ashes after she is cremated?" she asked as she tried to re-engage him into conversation.

"I don't know yet," he said. "Anyway, I must now go to the cremation room; they are starting shortly."

"I will come with you," said Lenore, as he followed him into the crematorium.

Chapter Eighteen

18 It was the worst kind of pain. Eli had never experienced pain like that. It was worse than his father abandoning them; worse than watching Justin waste away to an early death. The pain engulfed him, and took over every element of his life. He felt surrounded by nothing but darkness. He had hoped that there would be a limit to the pain, but the pain Zahara had inflicted upon his frail heart was inexhaustible.

There were fragrances of Zahara everywhere in his flat. Memories had become his worst enemy. He would look out the window and stare at the traffic and people going about their business. He would hear the little birds singing nonchalantly. Life was going on. After just a few days, the world had forgotten her; forgotten that she ever lived, and that she loved him. He yearned for her; he longed to be with her in death. No one could ever understand how much she meant to him. The one he loved was gone; now he felt like he did not belong. No one could see his struggle. The weight of the loss had crushed his spirit, and no one seemed to care. His mum might have suspected but did not know the depth of Eli's agony and he chose not to tell her. She was suffering enough. He wished he could take a break from being himself or even yet, he could be smothered by his own pain, and then he would be free from it all.

He had promised Zahara that he would not do anything stupid, but he often contemplated suicide. He even tried; but as he held the knot, all he could see was his mum's face – the hurt in her eyes; the disappointment. He could not bear for her to experience the same pain. The least he could do was die after her.

He hoped and prayed that Zahara would at least join him in his dreams every night; relive those special moments again. She did come to him one night. She stood at the doorway holding a burning rose in her right hand. She wore a black dress. She spoke but her words were muted, but Eli could tell that they were disapproving of his suicidal thoughts. She seemed very troubled, very unhappy.

The following day he had a call from a lawyer asking him to come to their office. The burly Afrikaans man hummed as he scanned through the paperwork.

"Ok, Elijah," he finally said. "Everything is in order, and fairly straightforward. The deceased left everything to you. There is a detailed list here, and I will give you a copy, and we will keep the originals in our possession for a minimum of twelve years. Amongst the items in the deceased's estate is a sum of R927,000 and a motor vehicle. If you can leave your bank details with my secretary, and she will arrange for the money to be transferred to you. I believe the vehicle is with yourself already?"

"Yes, sir," muttered Eli.

"Ok," continued the lawyer. "Ok, here are your copies. I believe there is also a sealed letter addressed to you. Be careful with it because I believe there is a disc of some sort. Go through the paperwork, if there is anything missing or not clear, ring my secretary at the first instance. She will give you my card. Is that ok, young man?"

"Yes, sir," Eli responded.

"Ok, that's it," he said as he stood up. "I am very sorry for your loss, my friend. But your loved one has left you a good inheritance; I hope you make good use of it. I hardly ever see black, um, you know people of colour leaving such inheritances for their loved ones but your friend was a clever cookie, so use it wisely ok? Buy a house or something." He walked over to Eli, and patted him on the shoulder patronisingly as he exited the office. Eli followed him out. "Cheryl, can you give this gentleman my card. Also get his bank details." He turned and faced Eli. He shook his hand, and said, "Good luck, Elijah."

When he got to his car, Eli sat down and wept. She really loved him. He bawled loudly. He longed for her touch. He missed her immensely. He looked outside, and the whole Pretoria metropolis looked strange to him. It all looked outlandish and daunting. It looked haunting without her. He felt so lonely and vulnerable. He could feel his tired heart beating rapidly, and he longed for her every being.

He was startled by the parking attendant who knocked on his window. "Brother, you have to move your car or put more money; your parking has expired."

"Ok, I am sorry," said Eli as he started the engine.

When he got home, he opened the envelope. There was a short note:

"Eli my love, I am so sorry but my tired heart is beating slowly. For what it's worth, I loved this place; the place that I was when I was with you. I did love every moment with you. For most days, I could feel my heart beating steadily; everything was clear; because of you, on most days I was me. But I always knew that happiness like that would never last. I knew that this place with you, as happy as it was, was never mine to have forever, although I hope that the memories of the great times we shared will see us through till we find each other again. Do not let anything fade into memories of the past, which is why I made this short video of you. It was the best moment of my life, barring none. I am conflicted because I hope you never forget me but I know life goes on; so go on and be the great man that you are destined to be. I pray that you will fall in love again. You were born to love. I love you so, and thank you for loving me like no one ever did. You stripped me naked and saw past my imperfections. You will always be my hero, my saviour. I know you have hard times ahead, but when you feel low and feel like you cannot go on, just think of me and all the happy moments we shared. A lot of people never get to experience that. Two hearts singing in one accord; you were me, I was you. I hope you will love again but selfishly pray that you never be free from my love. So, I hope to see you on the other side. I will wait for you. Yours forever, Zahara."

Eli tried to cry but no tears came out. He put his hands to his face, and sighed many times. Moments later, he put in the DVD. And there she was, beautiful as ever. Beauty in its most perfect form; untainted by the ways of this world. "Happy birthday, babe. This is a video that I am making on your birthday. I hope you will like it." He watched it with great sorrow in his heart.

It was from the best night of his life. He grinned as he watched himself making love to her. He thought his butt looked big. He felt weird watching himself, but for a moment, the world of pain was gone. He kept his focus on Zahara. He watched her open her mouth as she climaxed, and he felt the sensation that he had felt that night. He did not know whether to cry or let the emotions of the night past overwhelm him. He stopped the video, and slumped into the sofa. Hysteria took over as his whole body began to shake. He hated that place, that moment, and everything in-between. It all felt haunted and painful; nothing felt safe anymore. How could it not? She was no longer there.

He closed his eyes and wished he would die. He remained there until he eventually calmed down, and sleep took over.

Six hours later, he was still on that sofa, sound asleep. He heard a surreal voice. His eyes followed the direction of the voice. There was a shadow by the door. "You have to let me go, Eli," whispered the voice. "I am sorry, Eli but let me sleep sweetly; let me find peace at last." He followed the voice, but as he got closer, the silhouette would disappear.

"Zahara, please, don't go," he begged.

"I cannot stay," the voice said. "You have to go on without me. Stop crying yourself to sleep. Even if you begged or cried, is that going to bring me back? I will be with you in spirit until the end of time. I will see your face, I will hear your voice, and I will stay faithful. Goodbye, Eli."

"No," screamed Eli as he chased the shadow, and crashed into a door. He hastily picked himself up. He was deranged. Was he sleepwalking? "Hello? Zahara?" he yelled, "Stay with me, darling, please." But there was no response. He paced around the flat frantically. Had he really heard the voice, or was it all a dream? He looked at the clock; it was ten o'clock. He could not remember how he had fallen asleep on the sofa.

CHAPTER NINETEEN

—◦⫘⫘◦—

19 Loneliness engulfed him, and it drove his being into the solitary mind of a mad man. Loving her had been the easiest thing he had done in his life. The most rewarding too. Now that she was gone, he was shattered. Left alone in the middle of the four walls of their bedroom; a place when he had once sailed with ecstasy and flew closer to their angels. He could not fathom life without her by his side. Most nights, he was up thinking about her and crying himself back to sleep hoping that the tears would be the trail to bring her back. During the daytime, he daydreamed about their love, but still bottled his hurt inside in front of his work peers. He saw her everywhere; he saw her lurking in the dark corners of their flat. She was everywhere.

Taking an afternoon stroll through the busy streets of Pretoria during his lunch break, he saw her again. Eli was convinced it was her. He was sure it her wearing red stiletto shoes, and a long dress with a light shade of grey. He ran through the busy street. She could not have gotten far. The way that woman had swayed her hips was just like Zahara. He was certain it was her. He ran for at least half an hour. He stopped when he could not remember why he was running. His mind was hazy and distorted. Had he really seen her? So, where did she run off to? "Zahara, please," he said softly as he sat on the street kerb. People walked past him, and did not even notice him. "Come back, please. Life's just not the same when you are not here. I miss you; why won't you stay with me?" He sighed and stared at the busy traffic, and pedestrians laughing and going about their business. Life was indeed going on. Round and round the world was spinning, and he felt like a hopeless drifter. He felt his world twirling towards a huge black hole. He wished there was someone out there missing her as much as he missed her. Her brother! Mori! He should have asked for his number. He just wanted someone to talk to about Zahara; someone who knew her; someone to share the grief with.

"Eli, what are you doing?" a voice asked from behind. "Are you okay, son?"

"Ma," said Eli surprised. "Um, um, I am just resting."
"What are you doing downtown? And shouldn't you be at work? Lunchtime is over," she said as Eli stood up.

Eli hesitated responding. He knew his mum could always see through him. "Um," he stuttered, "um, I don't know, ma. I thought I had seen her. I am going crazy, ma. Please help me."

She looked at him and saw how lost her son looked. She felt a lump on her throat as hurt filled her heart.

"I don't know what to do, ma," he continued. "I cannot separate reality from my subconscious thoughts anymore. Half the time, I find myself pacing around the flat and muttering to myself. I do not know who I am anymore. Sometimes I feel like a demon dreaming. There is constant ache pounding my every being, and it is driving me ballistic, ma. Help me."

"Come home with me. We will pray to the Lord," she said trying to reassure him. "I will phone your work, and ask for compassionate leave."

"I need to get my car, and my stuff from the office," said Eli.

"I will get them," she said. "Let's go home now. You need to rest." They walked quietly to the taxi station.

"Do not let this loss trap and cage you, son," she said as handed him some aspirin when they got home. "Life is full of hurt, but you have to learn how to deal with it. That's how you become strong. Use your tears as a source of strength, and her memories as a source of inspiration."

"I know, ma but I have always tried to be good ever since I was little, you know. And you have always told me to do good so that my soul can last. You said if I did good, good would happen to me. So, what have I done to deserve this hurt? Many times, now when I look into the mirror, I cannot even comprehend my own image. I do not even know me anymore. I feel like there's something else in the background controlling me. Like there are ghosts lurking behind cursing me; demons controlling me. Sometimes, I feel so cold, cold from nothing at all; like my soul has left me. What did I do?"

"It's only a passing phase, my dear son," she said. "You are just in a hurting place; so much hurt and anger in your heart, Elijah. It also would not hurt for you to make peace with your father. You have too much heaviness in your heart."

"Don't go there, ma," he retorted.

"You asked for reasons, so hear me out," she explained. "The bible says for us to honour our parents. That's all I am saying."

"Oh, ok. So, I am being punished for not wanting anything to do with my wayward father?" he responded sarcastically. "I have lived my life trying to be better than him, and I am being punished?"

"No, no," she protested. "I did not say that. I am just saying you need to learn to let go of the past because it will weigh you down. That's all, son."

Eli remained quiet. Moments later, he said, "Do you really think there will ever be an end to my strife? All I have ever known since I was little is hurt, hurt and more hurt. Hurt when he left you and I by ourselves, hurt when Justin died, hurt when you got, um, became ill, and now this. Now I feel evil overpowering me and have no desire to do good anymore. I only see a dark future full of more hurt, and honestly, I wish death could take me. There are voices in my head telling me things."

She was stunned by his confession. She feared for his life. She began to understand the depth of her son's hurt.

"Maybe you should stay with me for a while longer actually, Eli," suggested his mum. "Come to our surgery, and I will ask one of the doctors to sign you off work for a bit. Give you time to regroup. Come to church with me this Sunday, and we can pray for the demons in your head son." Eli stared at her before nodding in agreement. He put his hands to his face as his eyes got teary. His mum walked over to him, and rubbed his head and said, "Even when I fail, in God I will still believe. Believe Elijah. No river is too wide, for you to make it across with God on your side. All you have to do is believe it when you pray.

Jesus is here for you my son." She put her arm around his neck as Eli whimpered. She said a short prayer, but even as she prayed Eli wondered why God was allowing all this hurt in the first place.

CHAPTER TWENTY

—⚬⚬⚬—

20 Eli tried to look to the future with optimism like his mum had suggested. He tried to clear his mind; went on many afternoon strolls, and tried to let go off the resentment he had towards the world and even his father, but then again, her love had been his asylum; a place he went each night to refresh his mind. Now each night brought with it darkness and its ghosts; shadows of Zahara still lurked in the darkness of his mum's house, and they kept him awake. He could feel her really near but that feeling disappeared every morning as the sun rose. Eli did not know whether to love or hate the nights. Even the slightest sniff of a past moment he had shared with Zahara brought with it the old, unhappy feelings, and stark reminders of all that he had lost and all that he had loved. It made him cold; it weighed down on his soul.

"My mind is drifting away from me, ma," he complained to his mum. "Is there any hope at all? Where is my God, ma? Can nobody save me?" he sighed and continued. "Where is He because I am sure if He was somewhere, then this hurt would cease somehow."

"You just need to pray, son. Just pray," she said.

"That's always your answer – pray, pray, pray! I thought God could mind read. All I want is for this hurting to stop," he said despondently. "My world has come crumbling down and all I want is for someone to help ease the pain."

"You should ask the good Lord for strength, ask him to grant you serenity to accept the things that you cannot change. Zahara is gone, son. She is sleeping with the other departed; let her sleep peacefully. In good time, the Lord will bring you someone else."

"I do not want anyone else. I am not ready to let her go yet," mopped Eli.

She looked at him, and hated that the whiny grown man he had become. She raised him better. He coped well with much worse tragedies in the past. She could not understand why he could not get past the death of that girl.

"Eli, look at me," she said with a bit of venom in her voice. "People are talking and laughing at you. I did not raise you to be a wimp. That is not who you are. You are a strong boy; you have always been. Stop your mopping and be a man." She paused and looked at his red and damp eyes. She felt she was being a bit unkind, but felt it was the bitter medicine he needed. "I always suspected that girl would be the end of your sanity. I am sorry to say, but she is gone, Eli and she is not coming back. Life goes on. When your father left, I could have drowned myself in self-pity, but I did not. I had you, I had responsibilities. So do you."

Eli stared back at her, but said no word. Truth or no truth, the reality was that Eli did not want to forget her. He promised her that he would never forget her; would never let go of what they had shared. "Death and beyond" is what he promised her. He so much wanted to die and be with her; he would be home again.

The following day, Eli voluntarily committed himself to a sanatorium. He wanted the voices in his head to stop. His mum was heartbroken; she felt helpless.

CHAPTER TWENTY-ONE

21

Three months at the sanatorium, and Eli did not mind the isolated life. The drugs seemed to keep him in a parallel universe of serenity and contentment; one in which Zahara lay peacefully next to him as he playfully tangled with her hair; however, as soon as the drugs wore off, the old feelings that pervaded his life would come back like an unwelcome guest. The chronic chattering in his head would yet again bring suicidal feelings, and his heart would beat insipidly.

Many evenings, he sat by the balcony staring at the traffic in the distance driving up and down the highway, and envied how they were going on with their lives. He often listened to the chit-chatter from the nurses' lounge. He loathed how they mimicked patients, and made fun of them. He knew they talked about him. They called him "Wimpy" but he did not care.

"He will be alright. He is just suffering from a bad case of heartbreak," one voice said.

"He is a sissy, if you ask me," said the another voice before a loud sneeze. "If you ask me, he needs to man up. I hear he is mopping over a girl who died. My brother lost his wife, and he was left with three children but he moved on, and now has a new family. That is what real men do."

"Hush your mouth, Kagiso. You better be careful about these hurtful things you say. People are different. One day it will be you, and we will see what you will do."

"I will not go into a madhouse, that is for sure," she retorted with a laugh.

"Never say never, my dear. Be careful, you never know what will happen when destiny catches up with you."

He hated them, especially the short podgy one, who always hummed tunelessly; but what he hated the most was how the world waited for no one. Couldn't they see he was trying? What was he meant to do with all the memories, with all the love he had for her?

Eli just grunted as the head nurse put four pills into his palm. "Care for some old lady's company, child," she said as she pulled a chair and sat opposite him. "I am Nurse Moloto, but as you may know, everyone calls me 'Mamaloto'. How are you feeling today?"

Eli looked at her and just nodded as he stared at the orange shades of the sunset streaking over the distant highway.

"I have read your file, son. I know you are here voluntarily, but these meds do not help you at all. These doctors will not help you; they will keep on prescribing for as long as your medical insurance is paying the bills. Only you can help yourself. I spoke to your mother the last time she was here." She paused to see if she had caught Eli's attention. She had. He turned and stared at her blankly. She continued, "I know you are hurting but try looking at the future, not the past. If not for yourself, do it for your mother. She is very unwell, and she is being strong for you. You know she will not be here for much longer, so can you at least spare her the misery of worrying about you being here?"

The mention of his mother's health struck a nerve. His dear old mother; she needed him, didn't she?

Eli cleared his throat as he sat back, before saying "When I was in high school, one of our friends, a very popular boy did something silly and was expelled, a few weeks before his final exams. We all felt sorry for him. I even prayed for him hoping that he would not get expelled but he was expelled. I did not think about it then but I do now. Do you know what we did less than an hour after he was gone? We arranged a soccer game. We hardly spared a thought for him after that. Do you know why? Because life went on. Honest to God, I genuinely want to forget about the past, but it is all I have. I know everyone has forgotten Zahara but I do not want to forget her or that we met or that she loved me dearly." He stopped as he tried to hold back tears. "The day of her funeral, my work mates went to the company picnic straight after the funeral service. Nothing even stopped. No one even cared that she was dead and I was hurting. Now all I see are nameless faces, and I realise how fragile I am without her. I realise now that the world is a cold cruel place, and all I have to comfort me are the memories she left, and the tender moments we shared. What is love if she is not here?"

"There is no one truth but only pieces," said Nurse Moloto. "I understand your hurt, but life is full of hurt and also full of love and happy moments like the one you had with her. Do you think she would be happy seeing you like this? Knowing that you are adding to your mother's hurt? The greatest gift you can give your mother is giving her all your strength even when it seems there's nothing more left to give. If you dare to love again, you will again find a happy place. Loving someone else does not mean you have forgotten your special friend. It means you are just daring to live until your time on earth is done, and you can be reunited with all your dearly departed. It is just destiny. Sometimes it brings the best out of you, sometimes the worst, but whatever will be, will be. Everybody climbs down Jacob's ladder at some point in their life. I have had my fair share of tears, laughs and smiles. I do not know what the balance is, but when I have been happy, I have been very happy, and that is what life is about, Eli. Life is about taking chances; you took a chance at loving her; now take another chance."

She got up, tapped Eli on the shoulder, started singing as she walked away, "Take the world but give me Jesus; Sweetest comfort of my soul…"

CHAPTER TWENTY-TWO

22 On her next visit, Ma Zwide prayed with him as she did on her every visit. As they prayed, Eli tried to visualise angel wings, harp strings and praying hands. He tried to find Zahara amidst all that. He could not but he heard his mum praying loudly and with ardour in her voice; she was pleading with God. "Dear Lord, we are trying really hard to reach you. Our arms are too short. Please reach out to us. Reach out to my son. You know where it hurts. Let him find comfort in you. Pain is overpowering him. Make him see past this dark tunnel; show him that you are still there with him. Be with my boy, O Gracious Father. You are just and merciful. Put your comforting arms around him. In your Holy name, we pray. Amen."

Eli just opened his eyes. He did not say "Amen". He looked at his mum. He could see the pain in her eyes. How she was hurting for him. How could he have let her go through this? She also looked different. Her illness was overwhelming her. Her face spoke of fatigue and pain. He felt guilt for his lack of strength. How could he have been so selfish? Nurse Moloto's words resonated in his head, "Be strong for your mum". He knew he was all his mum had. Just the two of them, just like it was when his father left. He knew that all that was good about him was because of her. She had been his rock.

"Thank you, ma," he muttered.

"It's ok, son," she responded. "So, when are you coming home?"

Silence filled the room. After a few minutes, he stood up, and gently said, "Take me home, ma."

"You have made an ailing lady very happy, my son," she said as she sighed loudly. "I know that when true love is lost, life can lose all meaning; trust me, I have been there. Like all that you worked for is gone; everything erased; but just like a blank piece of paper, you can start again to rewrite your stories; try to avoid same mistakes. I did not, but your father has always been the weakness in me; foolishly so. You my son will do better; you will find someone else to give all that love you have in you."

CHAPTER TWENTY-THREE

23 The priest's words echoed in Eli's head. "Eternal rest, grant unto her, O Lord, and let Your perpetual light shine upon her. May the soul of our dearly departed, through the mercy of our faithful God, rest in peace."

He did not know what to feel. He had been there before. Three losses in as many years.

"We beseech Thee, O Lord, in Thy mercy, to have pity on the soul of Thy handmaid; do Thou, Who hast freed her from the perils of this mortal life, restore to her the portion of everlasting salvation. May you grant your eternal grace to the sinners, and peace to the living. Through Christ our Lord, Amen."

Eli sat at the edge of the bench. He was too exhausted and drained to stand. Other mourners walked to him and shook his hands as they murmured a few words of comfort. Eli knew that most of the words were hollow and without emotion. Most of them had judged his mum all their life. He knew that even as she lay in her casket, they were still gossiping about her life and the ailment that had taken her from this world. He had never felt so alone. He was tired of looking with faith to heavens above. He was always felt that him and his mum prayed a tad too much, which made them blind to reality. The world was cold and mean, and then you die. He wanted to reach out to those around him, but he knew he could not. His mum was gone; and so was everything she had ever taught him – to pray and to dream. Perhaps, his mum's love had been the real asylum, not Zahara's.

Scarlett sat at the back. She had flown from London the night before. She was exhausted from the jetlag, but when she learnt of Ma Zwide's passing, she knew she had to be there. If not for Ma Zwide's sake, then certainly for Eli's sake. She sat there contemplating when the right time was to walk up to him and pass her heartfelt condolences. Her heart was heavy with sadness. She could see from where she was sitting that he was drained and tired, and out of his sorts. She prayed to God that he could cope. She knew how much his mother had been a constant source of his strength. She stood up, and walked up slowly and carefully ensuring that her heels would not make noise on the wooden tile floor. She cursed herself for wearing stilettos to a funeral. What was she thinking?

"Hello Eli," she said as she sat next to him. He stared at her blankly. He knew who she was, but he could not piece the scene together. Why was she there? Where had she come from? Was it real or was it another psychotic hallucination? Was his mind playing pastime tricks with him again? "I am so sorry, Eli," she continued after a long moment of silence. "I know how much you loved her, and how much she loved you too. I am really sad because I know she cared for me too. I am so sorry." She took his left hand, and clasped with both her hands.

Eli looked at her some more before eventually putting his head on her shoulder. "I am so glad you are here," he said and started crying again. "I am so glad you are here." They sat like that until all the people were gone.

CHAPTER TWENTY-FOUR

24 Scarlett had silent beauty with delicate grace. It surprised Eli how much he had forgotten that. Her face was always luminous with sincerity. She always wore half a smile on her face, like a child in a toy shop. Even the way she did her make-up was such that the tone was subtle. She always said to Eli that true beauty only needed to be a whisper. "Loud beauty is for skanks," she would say. "But true beauty beyond goes the surface; it is skin deep."

"You have been on my mind, Eli," she said rather suddenly the moment they entered his mum's house, "A lot."

"Really? You could not find better guys in London?" Eli mocked. He surprised himself that his mind could make jokes again.

"Up yours," she laughed. "I did date a few times but it never clicked."

"How few is a few?" asked Eli. "How many guys did you go through?"

"Jealous, are we?" she responded with a smirk on her face. "Eli, you are the one that I really want." She took off her coat, and moved to the couch. She continued, "This house brings so many memories. Anyway, you know me; I have never been a hopeless romantic or believed in soul mates or crap like that. All I know is that even though life took us apart, you have always been in my heart, and my thoughts. It is my fault, really. I should have never left. I should have stayed with you; you were needed here, and I should have been more accommodating."

"Don't be silly now," responded Eli as he sat next to her. "You did not leave me. We parted ways, and amicably so, if I remember well. Do not guilt yourself about anything. Things happened because things happened, you know. You had to better your career, your life, and I had to stay here for whatever reasons."

"I know, but I regret leaving," she said. "I should have been with you through your difficult times. Pure devotion to someone requires sacrifice, and I feel I should have done that; but I am here now, and if you let me, I will stay with you through the ups and downs."

"Are you sure?" Eli said, suddenly feeling a sense of relief and weight being lifted his shoulders.

"Eli, I have made up my mind. Never before have I been so sure. I am ready for whatever you want. Whichever road you will choose, I will go."

"And you are certain this is what you want?" Eli asked. "I do not want your pity; I get enough pity from the man in the mirror and everyone else around me."

"Of course, it is," she said and paused for a moment. "Unless of course, it is not what you want."

"No, it's not that; but I do not want you coming back to me because you feel sorry for me. Not saying that charity is bad, but if it is about offering a shoulder to lean on, you can always do that as a friend. I don't want to pressure you into moving back from London or anything. So, I just want to make sure that you really think about it, you know, why you want to come back," said Eli.

"Just say you are willing to give us another chance. We had been together for a long time, and I feel we really know each other. And I have learned a lot from mistakes of the past, from the things we did not say to each other. You don't know how many times I wished I had told you that I always felt safe with you, you know, and that I knew that I could always depend on your love," she answered. "My heart belongs to you. It has always been yours, Eli, ever since that afternoon you changed your plans for me. I missed you so much; I even shared a few nights with you in my dreams." She moved closer to him, and giggled, "I will be as loyal as a blind dog."

The scent of her perfume engulfed his nostrils and took him back to the zenith of their previous time together. He moved his two fingers in walking motion across to her thigh. He caressed her thigh, and gently pulled up her skirt. He slid his hand upwards and firmly cupped her chaste oyster. She squirmed a bit as the suddenness of Eli's hand took her by surprise. As he stroked her middle gently, she closed her eyes and moaned passionately. He moved and knelt with his face buried in her skirt. She lifted up a bit as he took off her pants. She felt the heat from his breath as his lips touched her vaginal lips. Her whole body became tense and expectant. After a bit of struggle, he eventually entered her, and she gasped as her whole body shuddered.

As he breathed hard whilst listening to Scarlett's passionate groans, it hit Eli like a comet. He realised what he had missing since Zahara. The touch of a woman; that sweet feel of affection, love and tenderness. Something to heal his hurt and take away his vulnerability. He felt a sense of belonging and a sense of life once again. He thrust harder, and Scarlett moaned louder as she signalled him to go faster and deeper.

CHAPTER TWENTY-FIVE

25 Two days before her passing, Ma Zwide said to Eli, "As sure as I am that I will leave this earth soon, I am sure you will see the sun again, my son." She was right. Scarlett was that sun; brought back by the tragedy of Ma Zwide's passing. With Scarlett by his side, Eli was confident that he could fight his demons; that he could fall in love again and he could even start a family.

He moved to England to join Scarlett later that year. A small private wedding, but well catered for, and two baby girls later, he was well settled into his new life. Everything had fallen into place. Darkness, cold, demons, fear – they were all gone. He had always feared that he would be a lousy husband and an indifferent father; but far from it, it all came naturally to him. He adored the girls, and Scarlett had seemingly healed the hurt in his heart. She had become a friend he could trust. He was glad that he had taken the leap of faith, because everything had fitted right in. Maybe God had finally heard his mum's prayers. Either way, he was thankful for his new found happiness.

"Six years and counting," he thought silently as he stood in the print room at work. He was excited about their planned getaway to the Scottish Highlands for their wedding anniversary. The girls were going to their aunt in London for the weekend, and they too, were excited.

"Is this where you come to hide from me?" joked an ash-blonde female as she entered the print room. It was Louise, Eli's boss.

"Of course," he responded with a wide grin on his lips. He looked at her and tried very hard to avoid staring at her chest. She wore a tailored amber flannel shirt which accentuated the swell of her breasts. He grabbed his copies and exited the print room, still grinning.

Chapter Twenty-Six

26 It was a bastard year; the recession was biting hard, and most people were verging on depression due to the financial woes. Money was not an issue for Eli's household. He had inherited enough from Zahara, and he also got a decent sum when he sold his mum's house. His own career was also back on track and had recently been promoted to Senior Associate.

But eight years of marriage, he started to feel life had become too mundane. Church on Sunday, dozing and nodding as preacher spoke often about what they ought to do to duck the wrath of God. Five days at work spent inside the confines of the four walls of his tranquil office were often followed by even quieter evenings at home watching uninspiring television. He started to feel like he was stuck in a rut. He loved his wife, his daughters; he loved family life. But he felt something missing; no spark, just existence. Sex had become a constant battle between him and his wife. More often than not, he always ended up the one with hurt feelings.

Routine after routine, and in between that, sincere heartfelt moments had become far and few; hardly any new memories. He often found himself in silence with his mind wandering about.

"What are you thinking about, Eli?" Scarlett's question startled him. "The girls have been saying things to you since we left church?"

"Oh, I am sorry girls," he said looking at them through the rear view mirror. "What is it that you said?"

"It's ok, daddy," replied April. "I will show you when we get home."

"Ok," he responded and looked straight head as the car revved up the hill. He was driving carefully. Snow had fallen that morning and settled.

"Ok, what's with you seriously?" asked Scarlett rather sternly. "You have been acting all weird even during the church service." She stared at him, and he looked back before setting his eyes firmly on the snow covered road.

"It's nothing," he muttered softly.
"Don't tell me you are still upset about last night?" she quizzed him further. "I was tired; how can you not understand that?"

"I said it's nothing," responded Eli.
"Obviously, it's something, otherwise you would have been a bit more cheery and nice to people at church," she chided.

"That's all you care about it, isn't it?" he responded with gravity in his voice. "Oh you were not nice to so and so. How about you being nice to your own damn husband?"

"Language, Eli," she said softly. "Mind the girls."
"Screw the language. I will speak the damn way I want to," he yelled as he cast his eyes across to her. He saw the blank look

on her face. She was caught unexpectedly by his raised voice and the anger in it. "You just don't get it, do you? Every time it's me who always has to mind this and mind that. 'Be nice to people at church; don't hurt my sister's feelings; don't do this to such and such'. When was the last time you were flipping nice to me, huh? When was the last time you thought 'screw nice', I am going to make my husband and my family number one?"

"Eli, please calm down," she responded rather quietly. "And it is unfair to imply that I do not put my family first."

"I did not imply anything. I said it direct. Maybe the girls, yes, but I certainly come last in your fucking world. I do not ask you for much. I pay the bills, I do not cheat, I am home every night, I look after the girls, I look after you. Damn, I am nice to your sisters too; love them like my own. And what do I ask for in return? That you also cater for my needs. Sex when I need it, which is not a lot, twice or thrice a week, that's not much."

"Oh, so it's just about S-E-X?" she said as she tried to belittle his complaint, whilst whispering so that the girls could not hear her.

"Not that same argument again! What the hell should it be about it? And you can say sex; the girls have heard it plenty of times on the TV programmes you let them watch. There are over fourteen hundred minutes in a day, and for the life of me, I cannot understand why you cannot spare ten minutes of that to attend to my needs? I do not abuse you. I listen to you. We have a beautiful house, and the mortgage is nearly paid up. We have food on the table every day. We afford decent holidays. The girls go to a good private school. We have no student loans. So, what else should it be about it?"

"Well, how about how I feel?" she asked with a crackly voice.

"Yeah, well, I have asked you before and I will ask again – share with me those feelings. I am not a mind-reader or a psychic. Let me in or quit whingeing about it..."

"Mommy, why can't you give daddy what he wants? You always give me and Skye sweeties when we want them," April interrupted. Her words stunned both her parents into silence. A few seconds later, Eli looked into the mirror, and said, "It's ok, honey. Sometimes grown-ups don't understand each other, and quarrel over little things. Just like you and your sister when you fight over the same sweet or dolly, but you love each other dearly, don't you?"

Scarlett remained quiet for the rest of the journey. She looked outside at the undulating white slopes, and the slumped tree branches poking through the snow. As the car went up the driveway, she turned to the girls, and said, "Girls, you go on into the house. Daddy and I will be in shortly." She paused as she took keys from her purse and handed them over to Skye, "You know how to open the door, don't you? Use this key."

Skye nodded.

"I also know how to open the door," remarked April.

"Oh, do you? That's my girl," responded Scarlett. "Go on with your sister. You can have some of those chocolate cookies we got yesterday; I will be in shortly to make you a hot chocolate. Be careful not to slip; avoid the icy patches."

Eli and Scarlett sat in the car and watched their girls carefully tread around the snow and icy patches. As soon as they entered the house, Scarlett turned and looked at her husband. She could not hide the exasperation in her eyes. "That was awful, Eli; saying all those things in front of the girls."

"I know. I am sorry about that," he apologised without looking at her.

"And why are you always blaming me for the shortfalls of our sex life?" she asked.

"Oh, we are still talking about that?" he questioned.

"Yeah, because I do not want to have this conversation again tomorrow and the day after that," she said. "Gloves off, tell me frankly what's eating you? If you want to find someone else to fuck, just fucking tell me rather than bash my self-esteem."

"Ah, come on now, Scarlett," he said rather shocked by her words. "I love you, you know that." He placed his left hand on her right hand, but she pulled her hand away, and looked outside the window. "It is unfair that you make such an accusation just because I said how I feel. I said those things because I want our life to be complete. All other facets of our life are in good place as they should be, but our love life is non-existent. And lately, it's becoming more and more routine, and out of obligation rather than, you know, out of your genuine desire for me."

"So, what do you want from me, Eli," she asked, still with annoyance in her voice.

"It's not what I want from you; it is about what is right for our relationship, for the girls. It's not good for any of us to be constantly fighting like this," he paused to clear his throat. "I have read somewhere that women withhold sex if other aspects of their lives are not well. And I ask you many times, is everything okay, and you say, yes, which leaves me confused. So, either you are lying to me about everything being okay, or you do not find me good in bed anymore, or there is something or someone else." He paused expecting her to respond but she simply snuffled. He continued, "Maybe it is the lack of creativity in the bedroom, but God knows, I fucking try. But you always hold back, and say those sex games make you feel silly. So, how else can I be creative? Tell me what you want to see in the bedroom. It freaks me out at times. Often when we do it, I last ten or so minutes, which from what I understand is good, but still it's not enough for you. When we were dating, all I had to do was stroke your breast, and you would exhale with ecstasy, but now it is like a freaking chore at times just to get you to make a sound. You make me look like a sex addict, but it's not like I ask for sex every minute or something. I request it when my body tells me it needs it. It is as much a physiological need as everything else like hunger or thirst, and if I cannot get it from you, what do you want me to do? That's why I get cranky and frustrated. It's not by choice… Google it or something; it is scientifically proven that lack of sex for men causes moodiness or something. So, I apologise for lashing out at you at times, but it's sort of a natural reaction. And that is the truth. I am not lusting after anyone or anything. I could relieve myself, and I do once in a while, but it is like playing tennis against a fucking wall. And why should I have to wank when I have you lying next to me?"

Scarlett remained looking down. Eli looked at her closely and saw the tears running down her eyes. He felt bad for making her cry. His mother always told him that he should never make a woman cry.

"I am sorry, babe," he said as he took her hand. She did not pull away this time. "I am sorry Scarlett; let's just forget it.

Maybe, it is just a phase; it will come back to us in good time."
But she kept weeping. She let go of his hand as she took wipes
from her purse.

"I am the one who is sorry, Eli," she finally said with a
crackly voice. "I am sorry I am not giving you all you want.
You deserve more, you really do. God knows I am trying,
Eli; I really am, but I seem to have nothing else to give at the
moment, and like you always say, when there is nothing left
to give, how can we ask for more. I don't know what's wrong
with me. I used to want you to make love to me all the time."
She snivelled some more as she wiped snort and tears from
her face.

Eli was stunned by the revelation that she had nothing else
left to give. Had he taken everything from her already after
just eight years of marriage? Was she going to leave him now?

"What are you saying, Scarlett?" he asked with resignation
in his voice as he leaned backwards. "Is this end of your love
for me?" He felt sadness in his heart, reminiscent of the time
Zahara broke up with him. He sighed as he rubbed the sides
of his face. "You want out, is that it?"

"No, I did not say that," she protested profusely. "I did not
say that. I love you, Eli, and even if I had to start again, I would
still marry you. I just meant that sexually, I feel impotent at the
moment; I feel dead like something sexual was taken from me.
And it is not you, God no, it's not you. You are a great husband,
father and provider, and I do thank God for you. It's me… I feel
like there is some demon within…" She started crying again.
Eli leaned to her side, and hugged her. She cried louder. He
squeezed her harder.

"I am going for a quick walk to compose myself," she said moments later. "I cannot let the girls see me like this; I need to compose myself."

Eli watched her walk away. He felt remorseful; he should not have driven her to that dark place that made her cry. She looked wretched and defeated. For the first time in his life, Eli realised that love was not a fairy-tale and would never be. He understood why people walked out of their marriages. He finally got some empathy for his father abandoning his own marriage. Marriage was hard!

CHAPTER TWENTY-SEVEN

27 "It's for you, sweetie," Scarlett said as she handed over the phone to Eli.

"Who is it?" he asked lacking interest.

"Don't know; I didn't ask," she said.

"Hello," he said hesitantly.

"Hello, Eli," said the male voice on the other end of the line. "My name is Jasper, um," he said and then silence followed.

"Yes, Jasper, do I know you?" he asked as he looked back at Scarlett, and shrugged his shoulders.

"No, um, no you do not," responded Jasper still sounding diffident. "I am your other brother, um, from Soweto."

Eli did not know how to respond to that. He looked at Scarlett again but with a blank face, before asking, "So, what can I do for you?"

"Father passed away this morning," said Jasper. "Our father. They found him lying on the veranda of a, um, a tavern."

"I am sorry for your loss," he said after a moment of silence. "But he stopped being my father over thirty years ago. I have nothing to do with that man."

Scarlett moved close to Eli, and whispered in his ear, "What's going on?"

"Nothing to worry about," Eli responded quietly, and shaking his head.

"Um, Eli, but he was your father. We are your family now," pleaded Jasper.

"If you are family, where were you all these years? I am happy with who I am; a fatherless child. Again, I am sorry for your loss, but I cannot do anything for you. I have not had anything to do with him for a long time, and that is the way I want it to be still. Anyway, how did you get this number?"

"But you are the eldest son. We were thinking maybe you could come down for the funeral, and help with sorting out his estate," said Jasper. "My phone credit is running out, so maybe you could call me back on this num…" And the line went dead.

Eli put the phone on his lap, and breathed deeply. "He is dead," he said without looking at Scarlett.

"Who, sweetie?" she asked as she stroked his arm.

"Um, my father," he said calmly.

"Oh, I am so sorry, Eli," she said sympathetically.

"Ah, come on now," he responded. "You know how I feel about him."

"But it's… he is your father, Eli," she said. "I think maybe you should go to the funeral. I am sure they want help with funeral costs, and it would be good to meet your other family."

"Yeah, right," he said derisively. "Now that he is dead, he is a saint, and I am supposed to feel sorry for his dead ass? What about his past wrongs?"

"You are supposed to forgive, my dear."

"Of course," he said. "But God does not forgive unless you ask Him for His forgiveness. He never asked me for my forgiveness. He never made any attempt to make things right. You think I did not think about it all these years? Lots of kids in our neighbourhood had estranged fathers, but they still visited once in a while. They still sent money for school fees. He never did squat for me. He left my mother alone to fend for us, um, and the things she had to do. The damage on her self-esteem; the things the gossipy folk used to say about her, about us, about Justin..." He stopped when his voice began to crack. He grimaced at the thought of his father now reuniting with his mum somewhere in the afterlife. "He can rot in hell for all I care. Do you know how many years I carried puzzles about him in my head? Up to this day, I wonder how my life could have turned out if he had not left my mom. For one, she would still be alive. So, him and his bastard family can all go hang." He wiped his eyes, and stood up, and exited the room.

Scarlett picked up the phone, checked the incoming calls register, and jotted down Jasper's number. She empathised with her husband, but over the years she had learnt to forgive her own brother, albeit just a little bit. She followed Eli upstairs, and found him inattentively playing a game on the computer. She put her hands on his shoulders, and lightly massaged them. He touched both her hands. There was unspoken compassion.

The following day when Eli was at work, Scarlett rang Jasper.

"Hello Jasper," she said calmly. "I'm Scarlett, Eli's wife. We spoke briefly yesterday when I picked up the phone. I am sorry for the loss of your father. What Eli said, um, do not worry about it; he is hurting too. What he said was not directed at you, so do not take any offence. Anyway, if you get a pen and paper, I will give you an address in Midrand, and I would like you to go and collect R6,500 there to help you with the funeral expenses. It's from us, from Eli, but you must let Eli grieve in his own way; do not try to coerce him into doing anything he does not want to."

"Ok, and thank you very much," said Jasper. "I understand what you said about my bro…, um, about Eli. It is a shame but I hope at some point we will come together. I have a pen and paper now."

CHAPTER TWENTY-EIGHT

28 Eli got home just as the twilight strengthened. It had been a long taxing day at the office, and all he wanted to do was slip into his loungewear, watch a bit of television and have an early night. It was over four months since the revealing confrontation with his wife. Things got better after that, especially after the passing of his estranged father as Scarlett offered solace to Eli's unspoken grief. But with time, things slid back to the normalcy of passionless routine, tension and few meaningful conversations. Scarlett was back on her script of headaches and fatigue. It annoyed Eli but he did not want another confrontation; so he became a recluse. He never pictured himself divorced; besides, he felt that he would never forgive himself if they separated because of sex. That would make him look petty or like a sex freak. He had to try to make it work for the girls. There were many sexless marriages around. Besides, divorced families often had it hard; he knew from experience; the scars stayed with you well into adulthood and beyond.

Scarlett did try her best; she tried to let herself go sexually. She even sent the girls away one evening, and greeted Eli at the door with nothing on but her silk gown. She had read it in a magazine. She felt silly doing it, but she loved her family more. They kissed at the door, and quickly rushed up the stairs. She pushed Eli on to the bed, and moved back and attempted a sexual dance. She loathed herself as she did it, but she wanted to make him happy. She had to slay the sexual oppressor within her but Eli noticed it; that her whole being was not in it. As if that was not enough, he also noticed how time had caught up with her body. The suppleness had disappeared from her breasts. Her stomach had stretch marks which bore testimony to the two pregnancies she had carried. He felt no sensation in his pants. He tried to engross himself in some sexual fantasies; but he was never one to indulge in such. The anxiety got the better of him. Scarlett advanced towards him, and Eli prayed for a miracle to get his soldier up and ready for action. Nothing! He still hoped her touch would awaken his senses, but nothing. She kissed his neck, his chest, his belly, as she undid his boxers. She stopped the kissing when she was greeted by flaccidity. She lifted her head with visible annoyance on her face, and asked, "What am I doing wrong now?"

It had been eight days without sex, and normally, Eli's loins would be fiery. Even though the efforts by Scarlett looked and felt mechanical and uninspired, Eli had never shied away from his bedroom duties, no matter the time or mood. It was then he thought that maybe it was not Scarlett's fault. It was just nature taking its course. Maybe the sexual side of their relationship had waned. It him hard; he felt that without that, maybe there was nothing else to strengthen their bond. Well, they still had the kids but what would happen when the girls became independent?

"I am sorry, babe," said Eli. "It's not you. Maybe it's me; perhaps wrong mind-set. I know you meant well, but I don't know, I would rather keep things simple. I felt like you were not yourself but that's not the issue. Maybe I have been too hard on you and this whole sex thing. Maybe, it's just time, nature; so, maybe our sexual side is waning."

As he said those words, Scarlett felt a sense of freedom. She felt the sense of obligation that had dogged her for many months shifting away.

"However, that scares me because, um," Eli continued as he stared blankly into Scarlett's eyes. "I feel like we are losing one important aspect of our relationship. It was the one thing that I knew I could do with you and only you but soon we will just be friends who have kids together, or maybe not even that." He kissed her briefly, and stood up to put on his pants. The sense of liberty quickly disappeared from Scarlett. His frankness instilled a new sense of fear and despondency. She knew if she let him go, she would lose him. He was the best man she had ever had, sexually and more. She had to fight for it even though she knew that her own needs had changed. Her mother had taught that successful wives and mothers went beyond their normal call of duty. "Difficult is not the same as impossible," she told her daughters many times.

She pulled him back with some brute force and shoved him onto the bed. She took his cock and shoved it into her mouth. The unexpectedness of his wife's actions awakened Eli's senses. In a matter of a few heartbeats, blood rushed down as his slumbering tool awakened. They made love hastily, filled with brutal desire, and it was beautiful. They climaxed at the same time as the heat from their bodies merged. Even after the shocks of the orgasms had died down, their tongues continued to kiss hardly. Later that night as they laid together, Scarlett acknowledged to him that their lovemaking earlier had been filled with excitement and intimacy she had not dreamed still possible. Eli smiled, and felt a huge sense of relief. They had not lost their 'yin-yang' after all.

CHAPTER TWENTY-NINE

29 Nonetheless, unbeknown to them, there was so much hidden pain in their memories. Eli had an inkling but he refused to accept it; like his mum had said, he had been given a new sheet of paper and he still had so much love to give. He loved Scarlett before Zahara, and he had vowed to love her after Zahara. And he did love her. She had found him in a dark hopeless place and bent out of shape. He owed it to her. She had been his heart's best friend before and after Zahara.

But there were no more new words to say, no more silly stories as they lay in bed, and many nights had no goodnight kisses. Their lives had become centred on the girls, and between running errands, they both often felt like shadows crossing paths. If their walls could talk, they would hardly have anything to discuss. They both knew it was a slippery slope, more so Eli. He did not want to go back to the dark days of thinking about the past. He knew loneliness would fuel empty thoughts; so he searched for inspiration. He was determined to find passion to fill the emptiness in their lives; he sought spontaneity as a panacea to their monotonous routines.

"Hi," she said as she kissed him on the cheek. "You are early today."

"Yeah," he responded as he took off his coat. "I told you I was going to come early today, remember? It was manic at the office today, so I left as soon as we finished the client meeting."

"I made risotto and trout," she said as she headed towards the kitchen. "Hope that's ok; I could not think of anything else to make. I have not yet done grocery shopping for this week."

"Yeah, that's fine babe," he responded as he climbed up the stairs.

Friday was movie night, but Eli could not stay awake. He felt his own body shutting down due to fatigue. He kept dozing off on the sofa.

"I am sorry, babe, but I can hardly stay awake," he confessed.

"Yeah, I know. You have been nodding off for the past fifteen minutes," she responded.

"I know. I am sorry. I just feel so tired, and to be honest, the movie is a bit of a snooze-fest, too. It is not really exciting," he said as he slid into a more comfortable napping position.

"Ah, come on, don't sleep," she begged. "Stay. I will make you a cup of coffee." She looked at him and did the puppy eyes look. She seemed very cheerful.

"You know I don't like coffee after nine. It will keep me awake for long, and then when it's time for bed, I won't be able to sleep, and then I will be cranky tomorrow." She motioned him to move closer to her, and he obliged. He put his head on the cushion and threw his right arm across her lap. He tried to open his eyes, but they were heavy. His hand softly caressed her hips as his eyes slowly closed. Then he felt that she was not wearing any pants, and his eyes suddenly opened.

"Are you not wearing pants?" he asked with exhilaration in his voice.

"You pervert," she joked. "I took them off when you were in the kitchen. I think I wore one of the old pairs; it's a bit too tight." She pulled the knickers from behind the arm of the sofa and threw them onto his face. The scent of womanly dirt on them roused his manly senses, and suddenly, he was wide-eyed. He sat up, and refocused on the movie as he continued to caress Scarlett's thighs and with more intent. He kissed her neck as his hand continued to fondle her thighs in expectation of moving inwards.

"No, Eli, not now," Scarlett said.

"Come on, Scar, just a quickie," begged Eli with eroticism beaming out of him.

"No, let's watch the movie," she declined. "I thought you wanted to sleep."

"Yeah, but that was before I smelled your pants. Come on sweetie, just five minutes, and you will be back to your movie in a jiffy," he grovelled some more as he nibbled on her ear. But Scarlett was not kidding, and her demeanour changed to categorically show Eli that she really meant 'no'.

Eli moved back a bit, and looked at her in utter puzzlement. "You are serious, aren't you?"

"Yeah, why can't we just watch a movie and enjoy each other's company?" she asked.

"Jeez, I was trying to go with the flow. Besides, you can record the movie or put it on pause so that you do not miss anything," he explained the obvious.

"Yeah, well I do not really feel like fooling around," she responded. "Let's just watch the movie; so maybe after the movie."

"You know, I really don't get you now," Eli said disappointedly. "We haven't had sex in six days, and you were home the whole today, and I bet you watched TV for many hours, and I am asking for just five minutes."

"I said maybe later," she said. "Why does it have to be sex when you want it? You are telling me you cannot just touch me and expect it to go no further? When we were dating, sometimes that's all we did. Sometimes I just want to cuddle, and nothing more."

Eli sighed deeply and loudly, and then clenched his teeth with frustration. "You know what? Watch your damn movie. You just don't get it," he said as he stood up to go.

"There you go pouting again. Ok, come on then, let's do it," she said as she opened her legs wide.

Eli did not look back. He exited the room, and banged the door in the process. When he got to the bedroom, he sat on the bed with thoughts running through his mind. For the first time in a long time, Eli wondered what his life would be if Zahara had not died. The moment he had that thought, he immediately regretted it. He knew thoughts like that would take him to a dark place. He quickly slipped out of the loungewear, and put on a pair of jeans, t-shirt and jumper. He wanted to get out of the house to get some air. He had his girls to think about; he could not afford going to a mental institution again or to get depressed. He did not want to be hobbled by grief again.

CHAPTER THIRTY

——◅◌◌◍◡◍◌◌▻——

30 He quietly headed out of the house, and walked towards the town centre. It was just over two miles, but he figured the crispy air under the crescent moon would do him good. He headed for the less popular pub in town. He wanted to avoid the rowdy revellers and binge-drinking youths.

As he sat in the pub, he struggled for thoughts to feel his mind. His phone rang, and it was Scarlett. He ignored her. How dare she ring him now when she could not spare him a measly five minutes? She kept ringing, but he put his phone on vibrate mode. He turned his head and scanned around the room to see who the other patrons were. Moments later, a redhead woman in her early thirties moved to the stool next to him. She looked voluptuous but she had pretty dimples and big round eyes. They had a hint of a shade of blue and they looked beautiful under the sparkling bar lighting.

"Gin and tonic, please," she ordered.
When the barman placed the drink in front of her, she remarked, "Oh, that is a big one." She laughed as she took a sip.

Eli smirked and muttered, "That's what she said."

"Sorry, did you say something?" the redhead asked.

"Yeah," responded Eli and cackled. "It's nothing. It was a joke. Not a good one either."

"Go on, tell me. I love jokes," she said as she turned sideways to face her.

"Ah come on. I said 'that's what she said' when you said your drink was big," he said.

"Sorry, I don't get it," she responded looking perplexed.

"Told you it was not a good one. It's a that's-what-she-said joke," said Eli, embarrassed to having to explain his joke.

Moments later, the redhead chuckled uncontrollably. "It's a good one," she said. "I did not get it because I have never had to say that's a big one in that context before."

Eli did not know how to respond to that, so he just grinned back.

"I bet you have a big one," she blurted out unexpectedly. She looked at him and winked as she sipped her drink. "I am Rhiannon by the way."

"I am Eli," he said as he offered his hand. But for some reason, his hand stopped in mid-air as he added, "Yeah, I do have a big one but I am told size doesn't really matter?"

"Nice to meet you, Eli," she said and stood up from her stool. "Tell me another joke. There is a free booth over there."

As they walked to the booth, Eli looked at her back, and noticed that she had a flat bottom. "Not my kind of bum," he thought to himself. As they settled at the booth, Rhiannon said, "Yeah, size does matter, my dear. Wouldn't you want an adequately sized tool if you were doing some DIY work?"

Eli laughed, and changed the subject, "How come you are here alone? Shouldn't you be with your girlfriends or your partner on a Friday night?" he asked as he checked her hand for a wedding ring.

"I could say the same about you, love! I wasn't planning on coming out tonight," she explained. "But my husband went out and left me with his old senile mom. I cannot stand the woman. She would not even let me touch the fucking TV remote control in my own house, can you imagine?"

"Oh, tough night," said Eli as his phone vibrated once again. He checked to see if it was Scarlett still. It was her sister instead. He answered.

"Where are you?" she asked after exchanging pleasantries.

"Am in a pub somewhere. I just wanted to blow off some steam," he explained. "Did she tell you she would not put out for me, her own husband? Nobody told me that was part of marriage!"

"I know, Eli," she responded. "I talked to her. Go back home, she is worried sick. You have to understand that maybe she is having some issues; it's just a phase."

"We all have issues. Remember I am the one who went to a nuthouse once," he laughed at his own insult of himself. "Anyway, I will go home when I feel it's time and not when she wants me to." They chatted for another minute before Eli excused himself.

"Tough night for you, too," remarked Rhiannon. "Sex starved, are we? Join the club."

"Yeah, something like that. I really don't want to talk about it," he said.

"Nothing to be ashamed of, Eli. Eli – that's a rather nice unique name, I love it. Anyway, I haven't had sex in over three weeks, and good sex in like six years now," she said. Eli looked at her with expectation for her to continue. "I have been married for nearly ten years, but now all that my husband does is go to the pub almost every night, and when he returns he fucking stinks of booze and whatever else, and totally drunk for any decent bedroom action. So, I got myself a couple of toys." She chuckled rather embarrassed at her own confession to a stranger she was seemingly attracted to.

Eli remained silent for a few seconds before raising his glass and saying, "Here's to sexless marriages." He laughed derisively. She laughed too.

"You can fuck me if you want," she said without warning, and the drink in Eli's mouth gurgled and he nearly spit it out. "I am just saying. No strings attached. We can go in the ladies. I know the bartender, he is from my estate. I know I am a bit chubby but hey a cunt is a cunt, right?" She laughed and continued, "Besides, who knows, mine might turn out to be the best you ever had. It is so wicked it would hum to you." She laughed, again with a trace of embarrassment. She always knew she was bad after a couple of glasses of alcohol.

"Um, thank you, but no," Eli said and paused. "But thank you. Really; it's just not my style. I have never cheated. I don't cheat really. I would rather leave someone than to cheat."

"What if I give you just head?" She placed her hand on Eli's crotch and touched his cock. Eli jilted backwards slightly at the sensation of someone touching it unexpectedly.

"Head?" he asked perplexedly.

"A blowjob," she explained with an alluring voice.

"A blowjob?" Eli thought silently. He toyed with the idea wondering if it really counted as cheating. And would they just stop at that? Would he have to do same to her?

"Thank you again, but no," he finally responded.

"Ok, your choice, governor," she giggled trying to hide the hurt of rejection, "Bad one, I must say."

"Let me get you another drink," Eli offered. "What do you want?"

"Make it *Sex on the Beach*," she said and chortled some more. "Well, one of us might as well have sex tonight! Anything with vodka please."

Eli returned with the drinks moments later. "So, tell me about yourself, Rhiannon," he said as he placed the drinks on the table.

"I am a nobody, really," she said as she tasted her drink. "Ah, nice. Now my turn to toast. Here's to, um, life sucks. Marriage sucks." Eli raised his glass but said nothing. "I am a nobody, Eli. You tell me about yourself, you seem like a nice made-up fellow. I am just a 'chav', you know, born and bred. I even married a fucking 'chav', too. I'm just a fucking housewife, and got three fucking kids sucking the life out of me, and a husband who won't satisfy my needs. That's me in a nutshell. Now tell me about yourself."

Eli did not want to talk about himself. He did not know her, and he could not trust her. She looked like the volatile drama-loving type. "I will tell you that joke you wanted," he said trying to avoid talking about himself.

"Yay," she said as she quietly clapped her hands. "I love guys who can make me laugh."

"Okay, but it's not a good one. I am not very good at telling jokes." He paused to take a sip. "Okay, one day this guy was walking to the pub, right? Then on his way, he sees a very thin dog, and he mutters loudly, 'Gosh, that's one skinny dog.' The dog looks at him and says, 'You could get beaten for saying stupid things like that.' Obviously, the guy was shocked. A talking dog? So, when he got to the pub, he told his mates about the talking dog. They said he was crazy but he insisted he was right, and asked them to come with him so that he could show them. So, they walked out of the pub in search of the dog. When they found it, the guy said, 'Gosh, that's one skinny dog.' But the dog said nothing. He repeated it several times, but nothing. His mates were annoyed at him wasting their time, so they kicked him and shoved him to the ground, and headed back to the pub. As the guy stood there dusting himself, the dog walked up to him, and said, 'Didn't I tell you that you could get kicked for saying things like that?'"

Rhiannon burst into roaring laughter. After a long while of constant laughing and banging the table, she eventually said, "Oh my fucking goodness, that is a brilliant joke. I swore I think I peed on myself a little there from laughing. Tell me another one."

They chatted for another two hours, occasionally sharing a joke and laughing. Still, Eli did not say much about himself; so they just talked much about nothing. He flirted with her now and again, and occasionally let her cup his crotch.

"I think maybe I should call you a cab," he offered. She looked drunk out of her skull. She mumbled something. "I said I am going to get you a cab," he said, this time much louder.

"I am ok, I could go for another round," she said.

"No," he said. "Well, I have to go. And since you have been great company, I would rather leave knowing that you will get home safely. Come on, let's get go you a cab; I will pay for it."

They staggered out of the pub.

"Thanks, Eli," she said as the taxi pulled in front of them. "You have been a great sport. Good luck with the missus." She paused and looked at him and added, "Have you ever thought about a trial separation, like taking time apart, make her miss you a bit? Or just leaving altogether? You are a handsome fellow, you can bag a nice chick anytime. Me, I would probably end with another chav, so I am stuck." She laughed. She hugged him and kissed him on the chick before slapping his bum. "Maybe, I will fuck the taxi driver." She chuckled as she tried to open the cab door.

Eli eventually got the door for her, and gave the driver a twenty pound note. "Take her to Wilmot Drive, I think it is right at the end of that old Council Estate before you turn left to head towards the city centre." He watched the taxi go before starting his own walk home.

When he got home, he slumped onto the sofa in the lounge. He was no longer as angry but still felt annoyed and cheated out of the marriage he deserved. He almost regretted not letting the pub woman give him a blowjob. Maybe the guilt would have defused the resentment he was feeling. Then he thought of Zahara's DVD. He had not watched it since that afternoon when he came back from the will reading. He paused for a while contemplating. What if it broke him down into tears? "Still be worth it," he thought loudly, as he went to the garage to get the DVD. It was hidden amongst his old stake of sport magazines.

There she was. Beautiful, leggy and her dazzling smile full of life. She danced sensually to high tenor notes of some Italian classical music which played in the background. Emotions rushed back and he wished the world had stopped spinning that night when he was with her. That was happiness that he knew would never come again; that feeling of endlessness. He paused the DVD, and stared at her eyes. He remembered the mornings when he woke up to find her staring at him. In that smile once lay all his dreams. He sobbed quietly for a long time before finally drifting to sleep on the sofa.

CHAPTER THIRTY-ONE

31 Eli felt like he was climbing down "Jacob's ladder" again, as Nurse Moloto once put it. He knew he was headed towards a dark place yet again, but felt powerless to stop it. He could never understand why things had changed so much. He never expected a perfect marriage from start to finish, but he did not expect a constant battle either. The transition had happened so quickly and without an obvious trigger; from the passion they shared when they reunited after his mom's funeral to moments of cold dreary conversations and very little laughter.

Rhiannon's words kept playing in his head. Maybe, they ought to take some time apart. He did not want separation. The thought of someone else taking his place in his home and playing with his girls enraged him. What if he went away for a while, but it would not be separation? He liked that idea. Just then, the girls walked in.

"Morning daddy," they said in unison. "How come you are sleeping on the sofa?" asked Skye.

"I could not sleep, so I came down to watch TV for a while," he lied as he hugged them both. "Come on, let's watch something together."

"Morning mommy," the girls said when Scarlett entered the room half an hour later.

"Hello, my angels," she responded as she kissed each of them on the forehead. "Isn't it too early for sweets? Have you had breakfast yet?"

"Daddy said we could have one each," responded April. "We had cereal first. I had Cheerios, and April had Crispies," added Skye.

"Ok," Scarlett said. She looked at Eli and requested, "Eli, can I see you upstairs for a minute?"

"Why did you leave me last night? And you did not even answer my calls? And when you returned at God-knows-when, you did not come to bed," she said trying to keep her voice down.

"What do you mean why did I leave? We had a row, and I need some air, some time to myself to think things over," he responded calmly.

"You have never done that before. I was worried sick; did you even think about that?"

"I told your sister I was okay. I just did not want to row some more, and I certainly do not want to quarrel some more this morning. What happened, happened."

"So, where did you go?"

"Let it go, Scarlett," he said with an annoyed grunt. "I went to the Pirates pub, and sat there for a few hours and then walked home and slept downstairs. You can go and ask them if you want."

"So, that's how it is now?" she asked some more. "We fight and you leave the house. That's not a good trend, Eli. We should always stay together and talk things over."

"We have talked and talked about sex. What else is left to say?"

"I don't understand why you always have to pout and get angry about sex? You just want it when you want it, like it is prescribed medicine. Or maybe there is more to it?"

Eli laughed sarcastically. "You make sex look like it's unnatural or deviant. Instruments are for playing, Scarlett. You do not buy a piano and let it rot and collect dust. You play music, and you enjoy it. That's what normal people do."

"Wha… what do you mean?" she stuttered. "Are you suggesting that I am not normal?"

"Is that all you are getting from my analogy? Really? All I am saying is you make my demands seem perverted. You make sex look like a massive soul-drenching and physically torturing chore. Newsflash; there are thousands of women who do it several times a night to make ends meet. And they do it with people they do not even love, and you cannot do it with the man you married and the man you purportedly love."

"What are you saying, Eli?" she asked seemingly bewildered.

"Frankly, I don't give a rat's ass anymore. Just do what you want. Sleep with me when you want or don't," he said as he stood up to leave the room.

"Did you find someone to sleep with? What is this?" she grabbed his hand desperately to stop him moving. She whimpered when he repelled her hand and exited the room. She followed. "Eli, please let's talk about it."

He turned and looked at her. He avoided her eyes; he did not want to see her crying. "Scarlett, I did not cheat. I have never cheated on you, and am not planning to. I will readjust. I will watch porn or whatever like other dudes. I will do whatever I can, but frankly, I am tired of talking and talking."

She snivelled louder. "Maybe, um, maybe we should seek help. We could talk to the Pastor."

"What's anyone going to do for us? Why embarrass ourselves by revealing our intimate details to that crook with a book? He will just tell us to pray, and then he will gossip behind our backs. We know what the problem is. I thought we were working on it but obviously not. Maybe it's just nature taking its course, so let it be. I am tired of us being lovers one minute, and then fighters the next. And I am not saying it's you; I am saying it is us."

"Eli, please," she grabbed his arm with both hands. "I don't want to lose you." He looked at her and the melange of sincerity and fear was written all over face. He felt tongue-tied. He kissed her on the forehead and walked into the bathroom. Moments later, Scarlett heard the shower running. She sat on the bed crying wondering what was happening to them. Why could she not be like her sisters and just give in? It was not him; it had to be her, she thought quietly. She knew that when Eli loved whatever it was, he loved passionately and extraordinarily, sometimes to his own detriment. She did not want for anything, yet she was seemingly destroying their matrimonial bed. She thought about how nervous and pensive she still got every time they stripped to have sex. In a way, she always felt lucky that her husband still wanted intimacy with her after so many years together. She remembered her Auntie Margaret complaining to her mum about how Uncle Jackson rarely touched her.

For as long as she could remember, Scarlett had always been scared of being lonely. Lately, she had been feeling so alone, and with each passing day, she felt as if Eli was drifting further and further away. She knew that once his frustrations had turned into indifference, that would be the end of whatever little intimacy remained between them. What if she woke up one day, and he was not there anymore? She felt cold.

Chapter Thirty-Two

32 It was one of those days. Eli had always felt that he had a sixth sense that told him whether or not he would have a good day the moment he woke up. The incessant strifes at his household were taking a toll on him but things were even worse at work, so he knew he had to be on top of his game. They had lost six clients in as many weeks, and the witchhunt had begun. Everyone was stressed.

He paced around the meeting room waiting for the rest of the delegates to arrive. He stared at the floor, and thought how much he hated the green linoleum covering. It screamed hospital ward. He lifted his head and looked at the framed blueprints the walls that looked like old advertisements on the underground train stations. Apparently, they were supposed to be inspirational.

The man from head office wore a grey striped suit and no tie. He refused to sit down. He paced around the meeting table, forcing everyone to turn their heads to follow him as he spoke.

"I need answers. I need solutions. That's what you are being paid for Louise," he bellowed as he pulled down the blinds.

"Poor Louise," thought Eli as he quietly shuffled the papers in front of him. She was a good boss. Everyone knew most companies were in the doldrums because of the economy, but it looked like the head office man wanted someone to take the fall to show that he meant business. Everyone put their heads down trying not to be noticed.

"As a minimum, we have to reduce our cost base to compensate for the reduction in revenue. So, I need ideas. At the moment, no one is giving me anything. Louise, it is your office, these are your employees, they need better leadership from you," the man picked on her some more.

Louise banged the table as she stood up. She stared at the man. Eli had never seen her like that. Her face very was red, and she was beyond enraged. "That's enough, David," she spoke rapidly. "You want to strip me naked and humiliate me in front of everyone? Ok, I will give you naked." She moved a couple of feet backwards and kicked off her stilettos. She began unbuttoning her shirt. Everyone stared in awe. Even David was taken aback. He was speechless.

"I have given this company every ounce of my blood and flesh and this how you repay me. I do not control the fucking economy, yet you are still baying for my blood," she mumbled on as she unzipped her skirt. She pushed it down revealing the supple curve of her hips. Eli felt an arousal and he could not believe it; he rebuked himself quietly.

"Enough, Louise," David said in a calm voice trying to be authoritative yet reassuring. "Enough, you have made your point."

But Louise seemed caught up in a trance. She bent down to unhook the skirt from her left foot. The sudden rush of blood to the head sent her reeling to the floor, and she passed out.

"Someone call an ambulance," requested David as one of the female colleagues tried to cover her. Eli remained sitting there, too embarrassed that people would see the bulge in his pants. He was ashamed for being aroused by someone's psychotic breakdown. Even more embarrassing was that he had secretly wished that she had taken off her bra; he had always lusted after her chest. "What's the hell is wrong with me?" he muttered under his breath. Maybe Scarlett was right; he was a sex deviant.

CHAPTER THIRTY-THREE

33 Eli knew he had to go away for a little while; Louise's breakdown was a wakeup call for everyone at work. The new boss said people could get unpaid sabbaticals of up to thirteen weeks, if they so wished, "to blow off steam".

Eli knew it was his chance to break the monotony in his life, and give him and his wife a chance to miss each other again. He still felt disgusted at the inappropriate lust he had felt for Louise. He felt like a sick pervert but he suspected that it was an underlying symptom of his troubled marriage. A break is all he needed. Money was not his great concern. Destination did not even matter; he was just wanted a place to go. All he needed was a convincing story for Scarlett. He did not want her to know he was leaving her for a while; otherwise, she would get hysterical, and the girls would suffer. Scarlett and the girls were all he had.

"I have some news, guys," he said as they were finishing eating their dinner. "Not so good news." He cast glances at each one of them and saw their attentive looks. "I am going to Switzerland for a while, with work. Eight weeks, maybe twelve."

"Oh, dear," said Scarlett with fright in her voice. "So, you could not get out of it? So, you will be gone for the whole spring, right?"

"Daddy, where is Swi… where are you going?" asked April.

"It's far away in Europe, stupid," said Skye.

"Hey, you do not speak to you sister like that," said Eli. "Apologise at once."

She apologised. "She knows I am kidding, daddy. She calls me dummy, too."

"Well, you should not call each other names, especially bad ones like that." He turned to his wife, and said, "Yeah, it sucks I know, but if we get the systems adopted quicker, I could be back in half the time. I will definitely be back in time for summer, and we can all have a nice vacation somewhere."

"Shucks," said Scarlett. "So, when do you leave?"

"In a couple of weeks' time," he said quietly.

Two weeks later, Eli hugged and kissed his family goodbye. He handled everything proficiently and with the same conviction he always had when he was going away on business trips. Scarlett had no reason to suspect anything. He had always been transparent with their finances. Well, almost transparent. Scarlett did not about the savings account with over one hundred and fifty thousand pounds from Zahara's inheritance. He was never sure how she would react if he told her where he got the money. So, every year, he always exaggerated the bonus payments from his work so that he could draw some of the Zahara funds. Money was never an issue for them, so

Scarlett never asked much. She was grateful that her husband was a good provider, and that their girls were in private school. She watched him go, and felt a sense of sadness, which is something she had never felt before when he left for business trips. Maybe it was because they had been fighting a lot lately. She felt lonely, and she hated it. She would be fine, she kept telling herself. He seemed sad enough to be leaving, so she consoled herself that it meant he still loved her. Of course, Eli felt poignant abandoning his girls but he convinced himself that it was best for everyone, particularly for his own sanity. He did not want to be like one of those sadistic creeps that were often reported on the news, who killed their own families before committing suicide because of depression.

"You take care, babe," she said. "You know I love you like no other, don't you? Don't you ever forget that."

"Hey, don't talk like that," he hushed her as he hugged her. "You wore brown pants with a black bow at the front the first time we made love when we were teenagers. I remember every tiny moment that I have shared with you. I will always come back to you."

"I know," she said as she squeezed him harder. "But kiss me before you go; please Elijah."

He planned to backpack through Western Europe, and maybe trek further down into the Mediterranean. He just wanted time out. Time to reflect on his marriage, and refresh his mind for the future.

When he arrived in central London, it was rush hour, and he hated the briskness of Londoners during rush hour. He decided to stay the night at a hotel near St Pancras Station, and take the Euro-train to Paris the following morning.

It was after 11pm, and he decided to walk back from a Moroccan restaurant where he had dined. The air was cold and crispy but he loved the City lights at night. He saw a gang of youths in front of him, so he crossed the street to the side. A few hundred yards later as he walked past a nightclub, he noticed two young men, one white and the other black, buried in each other's arms kissing. He muttered "fucking faggots" without thinking as he walked past them.

"What did you say, you fucking dick?" retorted one of them.

"I am sorry, I do not want any trouble," Eli was quick to explain.

"Uncle Eli?" asked the other one.
"What the hell? Aidan, is that you?" asked a perplexed Eli.

"Sorry, I have to go," said Aidan to his companion. "He is my uncle, can you believe it?"

Eli and Aidan walked to Eli's hotel without exchanging many words. They headed to the hotel bar, and as they sat down, "Aidan, what the fuck was that about?"

"Firstly Uncle, this is London, you do not go around insulting people at night. You could get killed," he said and then paused as the bartender asked them for their drink choices. "I don't know, Uncle," said Aidan, once the bartender had given them their drinks. "I think I am gay; or at least, I have been for the past four months or so."

"Four months? Fuck!" said Eli. "Who else knows? Your mum will freak out when she finds out."

"I know. I tried to deny it many times, but I think this is who I am. Other than the guilt of lying to everyone, I have actually been pretty happy in the past few months. All casual at the moment, and before you say anything, I am using protection."

Eli held back showing the feeling of disgust when Aidan mentioned "protection". How could it be? Innocent little Aidan?

"I don't know, Uncle," Aidan continued and took a deep sigh. "Perhaps, something in my childhood got me addicted to the dark side. I am happy though; it's mum that my heart breaks for. She will definitely say that I am now condemned right down to the most unfathomable depth of hell. And if she is right, that probably means I will never see my family, you, everyone, because you will all probably go to heaven or whatever."

"It's alright, Aidan," Eli said as he rubbed Aidan's arm. "Look at me, it's fine. I am sure we are all wrong about many things but we will never know until we are gone. Life screwed us all, albeit in different measures." He paused as he thought of his father. He thought about the many times his mum asked his father whether he would ever change his ways. His father always said yes, but all those times, it was always clear to Eli that he would always be the same. "I guess if you can show her that you are happy, then I am sure your mum will accept it rather than try to change you."

"I hope you are right, Uncle. But sometimes, it's so fucking hard to wake up in the morning, when your mind feels like it's full of demons pulling you to one side, and voices telling you to deny what you feel. Oh, man," he breathed out heavily. Eli could see shimmers of tears in his eyes. "When it all started, I would lie awake in my room, thinking about me being gay, and the shit with my mom, you know, my parents constantly fighting... um, I could not sleep and to be honest, weed, and a lot of it, got me through it."

"It's ok, son. My mum always said everything happens for a reason." He paused to take a sip. "So, what do you mean the shit with your mum? What's going on?"

"You mean, you don't know about the shit with her brother, Uncle Freddy?" Aidan looked up as he asked.

"Not a clue," responded Eli.
"Well, long story short, my understanding is that Uncle Freddy abused her when she was a teenager. Not just her, but Auntie Mavis as well, and..." he hesitated, "Um, I think Auntie Scarlett as well."

Eli was shaken by the revelation. He pushed away his drink as if he did not want it anymore. "What do you mean 'abused' them? Like beat them or have sex with them?"

"Not him, but I think he forced them to have sex with his friends for his own financial benefit..."

"He pimped out his own little sisters?" Eli interrupted.
"Yes, beat them too, and then blackmailed them, I think. I think that's the reason all three of them moved here, to get away from him. But now, Uncle Freddy has been here for the past few months, and he has made contact with mum, and threatened to tell dad about her past. So, in the end, mum came clean to dad, and he did not take it well, so they have been fighting a lot." He took a long sip, before adding "Now, their only son is fucking gay! Great!"

Both men remained quiet for a while, both staring down at the bar counter. A few minutes later, Eli raised his head and asked, "So, what do you want to do about this fucker who is terrorising your mom?"

Aidan looked up, and for a moment did not comprehend the question. "Um," he eventually said. "What can we do?"

"Any idea where he lives?" Eli enquired.

Chapter Thirty-Four

⋘∿∿⋙

34 The two men walked quietly on the footpath, shying away from the glare of the streetlights. They occasionally exchanged glances, but neither spoke. Eli tightened his hooded jacket collar.

When they were near the street with the construction works, they lengthened their strides and paced up to Freddy. They could both smell the alcohol in his breath from a few yards behind. Eli came up to the side of him, tapped him on the shoulder. As soon as Freddy turned, Eli punched on him on the nose. Freddy fumbled and fell to the ground. "What the hell, man," Freddy muttered incoherently. "Do you want money you thugs?" Eli and Aidan exchanged glances as Freddy battled to stand up.

Eli noticed the flicker of anger in his nephew's bloodshot eyes. He motioned Aidan that it was his turn to have a go. They had to be quick and precise. As Freddy tried to stand, Aidan's arm jerked out, and his clenched fist hit Freddy's jaw sending crashing against the construction site hoarding. Eli threw a follow-on punch, and it caught Freddy on the same jaw and slammed him to the ground. They saw his mouth wide open with drool over his cracked lips, and blood creeping down from his nose.

They had agreed not to utter any words for fear of being recognised, but Aidan went closer, and said, "You stay away from your sisters, you festering slime. You are no longer related. You do not show up at any event, not even funerals. If you do, that will be the last thing you ever do. Go back to South Africa, or wherever, but don't even come near." Freddy shifted and groaned. Eli moved closer and pulled Aidan backwards. He signalled that it was time to go, but Aidan still had some venom. He made a slight dash forwards and with all his mighty, he unleashed a ferocious kick. It caught Freddy in the testicles. He screamed and his whole body slumped to the wet paved floor, and became motionless.

Eli pulled Aidan, and they both dashed across the street and in the reverse direction. Their footsteps sounded loud in the cold silence of the night. They kept running for two miles until they were past the tower. The moon was a brilliant crescent in an azure sky peppered with shining stars. The two men used the dark alleys taking utmost care to avoid the popular streets and particularly the ones with CCTV cameras. They followed the stream uphill.

"Uncle," Aidan said as they walked across the car park of a retail park. "It's ok, right? I mean what we did? It's ok to seek revenge for the agony someone inflicts on you?"

"Of course," Eli responded even though he was not even sure himself. "You have to think of it as protecting the ones you love, and also who knows it might turn out to be therapeutic for you."

"I know. It's just that so many times I have prayed to God that if He made me straight, I would never sin again, you know, never do shit like this ever again."

"Everyone does that," explained Eli. "Everyone at some point seeks to make a deal with God, but we never live up to our end of the bargain. I am sure He understands. It's a cold world full of snares, son. Besides, do you think anyone can really escape fate? I think it has all been scripted already."

"You have not told me what you are actually doing in London," Aidan remarked.

"Can you keep a secret?" asked Eli.

CHAPTER THIRTY-FIVE

35 Eli again stood beside the balcony double door, looking out at the Parisian lights. He still felt dismayed at how his mind had become so fixated on sex. Every woman he saw, he played the "fuckability game"; a game they played during his adolescent years. He hated it. Scarlett was right. He wanted sex too much. But he was never like that. He used to be a gentle soul and considerate lover. Yet, he found himself overwhelmed by images of Louise's half-naked body as she suffered a mental breakdown. Still he felt sorry for Louise, the best boss he had ever had. Why her, why gentle Louise? He heard before he left that she was not doing well at all.

He took a large swallow of the cold lemonade and checked the TV for time. He was in no rush but he had always been a very time-conscious person. He still had not decided what came next on his sabbatical roadtrip. He had always liked the idea of being a recluse in the Swiss mountains. It was nearly midnight, and he could not sleep. He flicked through the TV channels; many of them were in French. He kept flicking until his eyes began to tire before finally closing them.

The room looked different, but he felt like he had been there before. There was an unsteady light in the corner. Next to it, stood a tall woman. She was maybe his age. He could not quite make out her face, but she had a luxurious look. She wore a simple white sheath, caught at the waist by a thin multi-coloured belt. She had a nice brown skin tone. He stood up and motioned her to come forward. She did not move. Instead, her hands slowly undid her belt. She held it for a moment before releasing it. The dress opened. She slid it from her shoulders, and it whispered slowly as it drifted towards the carpet floor. She stood naked, with a body that showed no signs of childbirth. She reached out her hands, and parted her long legs. He made a hesistant step forward. She leaned back as she moved her long hair to the back. Her nipples jutted upwards. He made another step. Just then, someone from behind said, "Where are you going, daddy? We need you." He turned his head. Sitting on the bed were his two girls. "We need you, daddy," Skye said. "It hurts when you are gone." And then the girls were there no more. "No, girls, wait…" he screamed.

He sat up. He was sweating. He ran his eyes around the room. He realised that he had been dreaming. How pleased he was when he learnt that it was only a dream. He got out of bed and went to the bathroom. What a lousy dream it was. A sexual nightmare? That was a first! What the hell was wrong with him?

He could not fall back to sleep even though he had only been asleep for three hours. He turned on the TV to watch BBC World News. There was a documentary about how Christians celebrate Easter in Israel. He watched as they explained the liturgical arrangements. He watched how the devout faithfuls gathered for the Way of the Cross in Jerusalem, some travelling from as far as South America for the Holy Week. At the moment, it hit him; Jerusalem was the place to go for redemption. He knew he had a better chance of soul revitalisation there than in the solititude of the Swiss mountains. He turned on his computer. There were flights available from Nice.

Chapter Thirty-Six

───◦Ⅲ◦Ⅲ◦───

36 He met Kaela two days after Holy Week. Three weeks in her company, meeting every other day, had gone by so quickly. And she had charmed him into him telling his life story. He felt vulnerable. He had told her things that he had never told anyone else but sharing stories from their past had turned out to be very therapeutic for both of them.

Kaela's companionship added a different perspective to Eli's stay and journey to self-rediscovery. Other than the companionship, her knowledge of Jerusalem had proven immensely invaluable. She had taken him to all the interesting Christian historic sites including the Church of the Holy Sepulchre and the Garden of Gethsemane.

Today they were journeying through the Dolorosa. Eli explained to Kaela that he hoped tracing Christ's path of grief and pain would at least help revive his faith and help him battle the inner fiends threatening to send him to the dark past. "Faith" was one thing that his mum asked him to never lose. As they climbed up the stairs, Kaela looked at Eli, and asked with a solemn voice, "Have you ever thought that the Devil want you as you are, but God wants more from you? Unconditional love, huh?"

Eli stared back. He had never thought about it that way, so he was lost for words. She was right in a way. She was often right even though her theories of life were insane. Her life experiences were nothing but ordinary, so he let her insatiably feed his empty inner space. They sat on a bench enjoying the beautifully serene views as they recovered from the visit to the Tabgha on the western shore of the Sea of Galilee.

"Not that I do not believe in super beings or whatever, I have never knelt down and asked any god for any favours, even when I was a little girl stranded on my own. Occasionally, I read the Qu'ran, the Bible and so forth, but only because I try to find context for the religious conflicts around us. And then when you hear the heart-breaking stories of loss and grief from wailing Palestinian mothers, you cannot help asking whether these wars are worth it, whatever the reason, religious or otherwise."

Eli loved deep thinkers, and Kaela was one. He could listen to her all day long. From the very moment she approached him in that dingy bar, they had connected on many levels. Their mutual interests extended beyond Arabic coffee and movies. It was also their past filled with grief and misery. Each day they spent together, their bond grew stronger as they shared travels and pleasures during the day. He loved the way she talked; she made him smile effortlessly just like Zahara did.

"I don't know, Kae," he said. Kae? He had never called her that. Why did he shorten her name? Sign of growing affection? He sighed quietly, and thought it was only a couple more weeks before he would leave Israel and return to England. "Um, sorry, I shortened your name," he babbled apologetically.

She giggled and joked, "That's okay, E."

"Anyway, I was saying. You could be right about what you said, but even Jesus said it was hard to get to heaven. So God's way, the requirement for faith is a means of selection through sacrifice, I guess. Wasn't it Ghandi who said 'religion without sacrifice is a danger to the human virtues'?" He paused and stared at her. He smiled, "Just like pleasure without conscience. As for me, I am just hoping to meet Jesus somewhere along this road."

"Pleasure without conscience, huh?" she thought loudly.

"Is that all you picked up from what I said?" he laughed some more. "Anyway, we should leave now." As they stood up, he lightly shoved her on the shoulder before grabbing her arm to stop from falling. She felt her insides flutter, and she knew she was taken by his blissful charm.

As Kaela drove them back to her hotel, Eli looked at her, and could not help admiring her valour.

"So, if you do not have a family, you do not read religious scripts and such, how then do you get through life's crises?" he asked.

She laughed. "I don't know, really? I just believe in destiny, and I have come to accept mine, whether this is it or there is more to come. Also, in my travels, I have seen diseased orphans, malnourished kids, child soldiers and the like, and it really does put everything into perspective. Ever seen a kid less than ten years old with 'nothing to lose' tattooed around his gun wounds. You think kids like that kneel up to anybody at any time asking for forgiveness or favours?"

"Hmm, but really, that's the extreme, isn't it?" Eli responded.

"You know it's only in the West, in the developed countries where people expect every aspect of their life to be perfect. Not many therapists and psychologists in the Middle East or Africa, right? Why is that? It is because people know that life is shit. It gives you what it gives you, and you make the best of it. Life does not owe you anything, but you people, not you, but you know what I mean, go through life expecting every step to be perfect, and complaining and blaming others when things do not go well. Like in America, I read an article about a Reverend who was blaming the white capitalists for the alcohol abuse in the black ghettos. He said the white man had put liquor stores at every corner of the black neighbourhoods? Seriously? Is the white man holding a gun? What happened to free will?"

"My word, I got you started, didn't I?" he laughed as he leaned over to her side as if he wanted to whisper something into her ear. "But do you ever think that maybe therapy, religion or whatever; all it is trying to do is take out the evil in people. And without evil demons, we would all be acting right. No wars, no crime, no black or white or Arab or whatever; just people, love and peace – too simplistic I know, but the point is that the world would be a better place."

She looked at him, and said "Of course, but you and I know that there will never be world peace. I hate the violence of course, but sometimes being peaceful does not count for much. Sometimes silence is worse than the violence. And to be honest, you can only push a man so much and for so long before he feels he has nothing to lose, and once that happens, the gloves come off as they say, and that is what has been happening in this part of the world."

She was quite vocal and bold with such strong opinions on many divisive issues. He felt like a coward for the many instances in the past when he had not said what he really felt because he was scared of what people would have thought of him. Maybe he should have stood up for his mom a lot more; his heart felt heavy with the words he had never said to his mom and for his mom.

CHAPTER THIRTY-SEVEN

―――❦―――

37 "So, what was it about this Zahara girl, then?" she asked as they entered her suite seeming rather mystified. "I honestly did not think that love like that was possible, that sort of devotion to someone."

"I don't know. She was just the one for me," he said as he took off his shoes before slumping onto the sofa. "For example, I am scared of flying like most people..." He paused as searched for words to elaborate his point. "When I am on a plane, I think about the possibility that I could die on this plane, and it does scare me. I guess it is the same for many people who do not enjoy flying. But the thing is when I was with her, you know, when we were flying together, the possibility of crashing did not bother me at all. I had no fear of death if I was going to die with her. It probably does not make sense to you, because dying is dying but as long as she was with me, I had no fear of anything, not even death, nothing. You know relationships have a tendency of growing old and cold but with Zahara, it was... um, you know, beautiful and divine. I often ran out of words to describe to her how I felt about her. All I can say is with her I had found something beautiful; it was wonderful. I loved her whether it meant something to her or not."

"Wow," said Kaela. "I wish I could feel the same. I mean I am sorry for the hurt of course, but it would be nice to feel that for someone, and to have someone that has sort of devotion to you. Wow, Eli. Wow. Now I see why you cannot let her go."

"I don't know, maybe I am just crazy like that. It's like those people who love surfing and swimming in shark-infested waters even though they know the dangers that lurk beneath. The passion makes you immune to the dangers, makes you oblivious to everything else, and with that much passion, comes the big risk of hurt. As long as I had her, I did not mind dying in the moment, literally. And if I could do it, I would do it again, because honestly, it was worth it. I do not believe that love is blind; instead when you truly love, whatever shortcomings the other person might have won't matter because love takes over – does that make sense?"

Kaela stared across at Eli as he spoke, and saw the blend of candour, love, hurt and strife in his eyes. It only served to increase her attraction towards him. "You were just whipped, my dear," she teased.

Eli laughed. "That is not to say I do not love Scarlett. I do love my wife, but it is different. With Zahara, I literally smiled every time. I was so contented. I felt bubbly; I felt dizzy as a fool, um, I was just so blissfully happy, you know. Anyway, that was then. Now I have a different perspective, or I am trying to find a different perspective because that kind of passion gives you lifetime demons, you know. One thing I have learnt though is that you may be around tomorrow, but your dreams might not be." He sighed as he scratched his left cheek. "Anyway, I got to go, it's getting late," he said as he stood up. "So, yeah, you can kiss me goodnight." He walked over to Kaela, who was stood next to the window. He put his hand to the side of her waist, and kissed her on the cheek. "Goodnight Kae...la. Great company as usual. You should become a tourist guide and escort rolled in one!"

Without warning, Kaela turned her head and let her supple lips touch Eli's. She put her hands around his neck and kissed him. The surprise element stirred Eli's senses like an adrenaline shot. He kissed her back for a while before he stepped away from her.

"Oh, shit," he said. "Oh fuck. Sorry Kaela, but I can't do this. We cannot do this... we should not do this." He hurried to the table and grabbed his phone. He sighed as his endorphins raged. Kaela followed him and pleaded with an erotic voice, "Please Eli. Just this once. Give me your passion. Just meaningless sex between friends, please; you know, the friends with benefits thing, please."

Eli grabbed his coat and shoes, and made a hasty exit. He could hear the pounding of his heart. He hurried down the stairs, and when he got down to the foyer, he turned back as if he was expecting Kaela to be behind him. He paused to catch his breath.

"Are you ok, sir?" asked the hotel receptionist. "Do you need a taxi again today?"

"Yes. No, no, not now," he responded. "Um, where is your bar?"

"Through those double doors," she said. "Have a good evening, sir. Let me know when you want me to call you a taxi." She knew he was a good tipper.

He made his way to the bar, and ordered half a pint of lemonade. He could not think straight. He had not thought of Kaela that way; well, he had but only for a short moment in the first few days of meeting her. All she had been for the past three weeks was a witty holiday companion, and a guide around Jerusalem. He knew that her opinions were often insane, but her wicked sense of humour always blew his mind away.

Now the kiss had made him feel things he had not felt for a long time. It awakened things that had been lying beneath. His endorphins continued to rage. The kiss had a promise of passion, but Eli knew that would be derailing his hard walk to redemption. He put his hands on his head, and breathed out loudly. "Are you ok, sir?" asked the bartender.

"Yeah, I am good. Thank you. Just a rough night," he responded. "Um, can I actually have two shots of vodka, please?"

He downed the two shots, and with each shot, he lost his fear and rationality. He had not had alcohol since his depression following Zahara's untimely death. He knew he was getting his defences down, and that was only going to lead to a trail of sin.

"Another one, please," he said to the bartender. He always said that the road to redemption had no set directions, but at that moment he wished the road was paved and made, with signs along the way.

Chapter Thirty-Eight

38 He knocked at the door. He looked at his watch as if he was counting the seconds. He tried to keep his mind distracted from the reality of what he was about to do. Kaela opened the door, and moved back a couple of steps. There were no questions to be asked; no words to be spoken. Eli knew he was crossing the line of fidelity for the first time in his life. He tried not to think about life beyond that.

Kaela had waited for that moment for such a long time. She gazed at him, and motioned him to close the door. She turned and walked towards the window. She felt a buzz running through every part of her loins. She was shocked by the intensity of her own desire.

Eli stared at her back, and made her rounded buttocks through the translucent gown. He closed the door and remained motionless. His throat felt dry so he tried to swallow some saliva. It made a sound as if he was about to speak. Kaela turned and looked at him but said no word. He walked softly to her, and gently slid the gown to the floor. He gasped at the sight of Kaela's nude body. It was nearly eleven weeks since he was last intimate with a woman.

She quickly undid his trousers as he took off his shirt, and for a moment, they both stared at each other's nakedness.

"Gracious goodness, you are gorgeous Eli," Kaela whispered.

Eli moved closer and held her cheeks as he kissed her. Kaela tensed when Eli's hands moved towards her bum, but it only lasted for a fraction of a second before she relaxed and let his tender hands caress her body. When he kissed her breasts, she felt her own nipples harden, and she trembled. She grabbed on to his back for support as they moved towards the bed.

They made love slowly and beautifully. It had been a very long time since Eli had felt such sensation. She moved her lips softly and breathed his name. Her mind was being blown away in immeasurable proportions; it was her first experience of the real intimate face of sex, and she loved it. She felt fire within her loins and so much desire in her heart. Spinning on that edge of sexual satisfaction, she kissed his lips, and thought of all the many different ways to make him burn under her spell. Her heart sang like a philharmonic choir. She wanted to drown him with her unrelenting passion; make him form new memories. She knew he was broken inside, but she thought silently, "Nobody's perfect." She yearned to fill him with laughter and ecstasy, but even in that moment, she knew she was on borrowed time with him. He would never stay forever to be with her. There was never going to be a happy ending. Would he even stay the night? She did not care; she just wanted him to hold her until the feelings in her subsided.

CHAPTER THIRTY-NINE

39 She looked at Eli, and felt the flutter of her whole body. She hated that he made her feel that way, yet he could not even see it. Why could he not see that she was so in love with him?

"Why are you still hung up on that dead girl? Why won't you notice that I am in love with you? Can't you forget the past, and simply be mine?"

"Because I am fucking married, that's why," he responded.

"Well, you are here with me, aren't you? Here in this godforsaken place," she blurted out. "Didn't you say earlier today that what you have learnt in life is that you may be around tomorrow, but your dreams might not be? Or was that just talk?"

She had found love in him, in the most unusual place. She was smitten with his infectious smile and ragged looks. From day one, he had spoken like he had always known her; but she was mostly in love with his vulnerability; his hurt soul. She felt she was worthy of his love; worthy to be held in his arms. She had kissed his lips, and they were full of passion. She was in love with all of him, even the demons within.

"We are strange as angels in a troubled land and the only thing we have is finding comfort in each other. I have been so alone all my life, but I have found serenity with you. I can heal your hurt. Look, you came out here to find yourself, to find a meaning for your troubled soul. I can give you that meaning. I know how fragile you are. I will give you whatever you want. Just give me a chance to heal the hurt. You will never know if you never try," she pleaded.

"Kaela, please do not throw yourself like that in front of me. What you think I am to you is not real. I kissed your mouth, made love to you; that's all we needed in that moment. It was just sex. Our defences were weak, we got lost in the moment. Let's leave it at that," he responded trying to instil boldness into his voice.

"I do not believe you. It was not just sex. You are trying to build miles and miles of artificial mountains between us. You are trying to hang on to that dead girl. You are masking your true feelings. Let her go, and let me in," she said. "Love is right within our grasp; something great within our reach. Just give me the chance to be your one and only. Eli, you are always free to make a choice, just open your eyes and see what's in front of you. Am I not the one you have been telling your fears to in the past few weeks?"

Eli paused for a moment. He sighed and said, "It's not about what I feel. It's about what's right." He left the sentence hanging. He did not know what else to say. He grabbed his coat, and made for the exit.

Kaela yelled "Eli stop! Please don't go. Why do you keep running away? What are you afraid of? Fear is such a weak emotion. You seem scared of almost everything, even afraid to face the truth that you and that girl will never be. She is gone. I bet you are even scared of your feelings towards me. I have been alone all my life, please, I deserve this. Give me a chance."

Kaela tried to make a desperate last stand. She held his cheeks and kissed him passionately. She felt him respond. She desperately wanted him. But a few seconds later, Eli stepped back and said, "Let go off my hand. Kiss me no more; this is a mistake and you know it. For my part, I am truly sorry." He shut down the door, and took a deep breath. He wanted to get away as fast as his legs could carry him. He did not want to have time to think about his feelings. He knew it was a mess inside his head, and probably inside his heart too, but that was neither the time nor the place to clean out the closet.

Kaela lied on the bed, and huddled herself into a foetal position. Ever since she left her parents, she had never allowed herself to be vulnerable. She had never given herself the strength to address her emotions; the strength to cry. But when Eli shut the door, her emotions shook to pieces. Tears started rolling down her eyes. She got hysterical. She cried and cried as deep sorrow filled her heart, soul and every part of her. She had been on the road for fifteen years all by herself, with no shoulder to lean on. Fifteen years of many nights with lonesome silence. But the past three weeks with Eli had been the best moments of those fifteen years. He had made her realise that she too could fly. He showed her new possibilities in love, and now she had fantasies of what love could really be. She did not want to live a lie anymore. She was now scared of being lonely. She was tired of running. She had run out of places to hide. She wanted somebody to love and to love her back. Someone to offer a simple sincere gesture, to whisper a sweet word into her ears every night. Someone to tell her she was beautiful. She wanted Eli. She desperately wanted him to take her away; to save her from her own ghosts from days past that also lurked in the dark, and be a guide for her many walks through the darkness. She remembered how they made love, and how beautiful every second of that moment had been. The caress of men always numbed her body, but not Eli's hands. That's why he was beautiful in her eyes. She wept uncontrollably until her eyes were red and puffy. But no one was there to save her; no one to notice her hurt as she quietly hummed in Arabic, *"Love continues to evade me, yet I am a sincere woman; From where the palm tree grows; Before I die, I hope to share all the love in my heart. Instead, I continue to sing verses about tales of my robbed innocence."*

As she lay there, she thought about when Eli told her that there had to be a place better than this world. A place where we would meet all the loved ones we lost. She told him she did not have anyone that she wanted to meet again; but now she could feel it. She understood what he meant. She wanted him, in this life and beyond. She cried some more.

CHAPTER FORTY

40 As Eli walked towards the boarding gate in Terminal 3 at Ben Gurion International Airport, his mobile phone rang. It was Kaela. He hesitated to answer. Eventually, he answered, "Hello."

"Eli, it's Kaela," she said. "I am sorry about what I said last night. Emotions were running high, I am really sorry. Can I see you please?"

Eli remained silent. A female voice on the tannoy announced "Flight to Nice now boarding. Passengers please proceed to boarding gate."

"Eli, where are you?" quizzed Kaela in a frenzied voice. "Eli, you are leaving, aren't you? Oh my goodness, Eli, I said I was sorry."

"I am sorry too," responded Eli. "I am sorry but I think this is for the best."

"Eli, I cried all night. I felt lonely. I am sad Eli. I hurt too. Please, stay for a bit. I will not ask for more. I loved your company; it soothed me. Please stay," she begged ardently with a broken tone in her voice. Eli took a deep breath and sighed, but said nothing. "Eli, I am sorry for throwing myself in front of you like I did. But for a long time, I have felt like I have been standing outside heaven waiting for God or an angel or someone to come and get me. Then you came along, and that feeling was gone. That is why I hurled myself in front of you like that. I am sorry. Just stay please. I just want to be with you," she paused before emphasising, "As a friend. Please, Eli. I need you here. I am drowning in hurt and loneliness. Please."

Eli sensed the hurt in Kaela's voice. It had been enchanting for him too playing with Kaela's heartstrings, but now the thoughts of his daughters were all that lingered in his mind. He had not realised how much he missed them. He wanted to go home where he knew the sounds of their voices would mellow him. He knew he did not belong in this place, certainly not with Kaela. Thoughts flickered in his mind. "I am sorry, Kaela. I really am," he said eventually. "Maybe I will come back. Maybe I will call. I need to go home. For what it is worth, you are a great woman. Ever since I met you, you were a great friend to me even though you did not know me. Under different circumstances, I would give you my heart, all of my love. I would. I am so sorry."

She had always hoped that there was love waiting for her on the top of some distant hill, but now it seemed that too was just a lie, an illusion. Her heart pounded with sadness she had never known before. It killed her that she loved him. She regretted letting her guard down and allowing him in. She hated the gods for toying with her heart; with her emotions. How could she have been in so deep, so quickly? Why did she have to fall in love with him? Why did she let her guard down after all those years? She was tired of being lonely; the hidden misery was gradually sucking life out of her. She knew that unsettled hearts promised what they could not deliver but she did not mind being miserable with him.

"Damn you, Eli," she said with a crackly voice as she popped open a bottle of wine. She drank straight from the bottle and wondered if it was time for her to ask for a favour from the gods above. It had been a long time. She had not bent down in prayer in ages but without hesitation, she fell to the ground and bowed her head. She steadied still her doubts before asking for the one thing she desired the most. Love! Love! Love! The one gift that had evaded her all her life; the one feeling that preceded bliss. All she wanted to do was play him the gentle symphonies hidden in her troubled heart.

CHAPTER FORTY-ONE

41   He kept reminding himself that yesterday was gone. And with it, the bittersweet delinquent moments with Kaela. He was a better man now. He knew what he wanted in life. It was a "til-death-do-us-part" life with Scarlett, watching their girls grow. Their relationship was going to be better; no more emotional bruises on each other. Still, he felt unconvinced that the guilt that he felt deep within was not written all over his face. Kaela's cries resonated in his head. How could he have been so heartless? Perspiration prickled like pinheads under his armpits. He opened his arms slightly as he made the turn into his street. The crescent moon lit the dead quiet street. He looked forward to watching the girls riding their bikes up and down the street. "Home sweet home," he muttered as turned into the driveway. He climbed out and stood and looked around. He immediately noticed how overgrown the weeds on their elderly neighbour's front garden were. He wondered whether she had finally crocked. But surely Scarlett would have told him when they had last spoken on the phone. It was nearly eleven thirty, and for a Friday night, their suburban street was as still and as silent as a town under wartime curfew. He grabbed his bags and gently closed the doors. He noticed a bit of moss and mould on the paving slabs, and thought that would be his first gardening task the following day. He pressed the door buzzer, and waited; a wide grin on his face. He knew Scarlett would tell him off for waking up the girls but he did not care. He was happy to be home.

"Were you expecting anyone else?" a male voice asked. He immediately recognised the voice. He instinctively turned, with his eyes searching. There it was. Carl's car, parked on the street thirty yards away from their driveway. He had not seen it. What was Carl doing there? "Who is it?" asked the voice on the other side of the door.

"Open the door, you idiot. It's my fucking house," said Eli, his temperature ever rising.

The door swung open. Carl stood to the side of the doorway, with a glass of wine in his hand. Half of the buttons on his shirt were unbuttoned, and the sleeves were rolled up, showing his muscles.

"Home at last," muttered Carl rather awkwardly. He placed the wine glass on the front porch window sill and offered Eli help with the bags, but Eli ignored him, and remained motionless.

He looked at Scarlett standing in the hallway. She looked different; beautifully different. She wore a turquoise silk dress that accentuated her silhouette. She wore no bra, and if he moved any closer, he would almost see her dark nipples under the sheer silk material. He could tell that she had lost weight.

She looked good, very good. Her hair was piled casually on her head, and the hallway light gave it an exuberant shine.

"Eli," she said hesitantly and visibly shocked to see him. Eli stepped inside, and put down the bags. He peered around; nothing had changed. The girls' favourite coats were on the hanger as they often were. There were cobwebs on the one of the hallway lights. He moved forward and brushed the cobwebs with his keys. Both Scarlett and Carl did not know what to say or where to move to.

"Aren't you pleased to see me, dear wife?" he asked rhetorically.

"Eli, it's not what you think," Carl blurted out.
"Oh, is that right? What am I thinking, dear friend?" Eli responded with a raised agitated voice.

"Eli, maybe you have had a long journey, but you need to calm down," said Carl.

"Calm down? Calm down?" he repeatedly asked as he advanced towards Carl. "I find you in my fucking house, doing whatever, and drinking wine with my fucking wife, and you tell me to fucking calm down. Where the hell do you get off, you pill-popping slimy son of a bitch?"

"Eli, please", pleaded Scarlett, even though she did not know what was going to happen next. They had done nothing wrong, but it did not look that way, and it certainly did not feel that way. All the same, Eli stopped when his wife spoke. He looked at her, and saw the fear in her eyes.

Eli looked at his friend, and hated the smug look on his face. He moved forward as his fist lashed in a wide curving arc. At the corner of his right eye, he caught a glimpse of Carl falling hurtling towards the staircase timber handrail. His cheek bone hit the rail post first, before he landed on the barrier matting with face first.

Scarlett screamed. At that moment, Eli remembered the girls. "Oh, shit," he murmured as he rubbed the back of his hand. "Are the girls sleeping?" he asked.

Scarlett visibly scared out of her wits, shook her head, before saying, "They are at a sleepover at Jenny's house."

"Oh my days, so you had the whole fucking house to yourselves," he said as he leaned against the wall and continued to rub his hand.

"You idiot, you broke my fucking nose," complained Carl as he stood up. "You fucking animal, you are going to pay for this." But Eli's reasoning was shut off behind the cloud of loathing. He leapt forward and kicked Carl in the groin. Scarlett yelled but her voice was drowned by Carl's roar of pain.

"Get the hell out of my house, you backstabbing scum," screamed Eli. "Go to the police or whatever, I don't care. Just get the hell out of here before I send you to the emergency room. Just because your own marriage failed, you want to ruin mine? And you are supposed to be my buddy? Aargh!"

"Eli, please I am begging you. Nothing happened," Scarlett begged with her arms crossed and rubbing her own shoulders as if to comfort herself. "I am sorry, Eli. I did not know you were coming today."

Eli rebuffed her. "Whatever! So, it is my fault for not telling you when I was coming home? It's too much for a man to come to his home and expect no one but his wife and kids to be waiting for him?" He moved past a kneeling Carl, shoving him slightly, and went up the stairs still mumbling. Scarlett slid down the wall with her back against it. She was sobbing.

Twenty minutes later, after Carl had limped away, Scarlett followed up the stairs and went into the bedroom. Eli was not there. She could hear him playing some music in the study room. Her heart shook with pain. Was this the end of her life as she knew it? She sobbed some more.

Eli sat in front of the computer with his hands on his head. The soft music playing sounded very distant. He had not anticipated this. All he had ever thought about on the journey back was a new beginning. He wanted to leave yesterday's ghosts in the past where they belonged; little did he know he would be walking into a new nightmare – one of his best friends getting tipsy and cosy with his wife. What if they had done it before? But the uneasiness between them suggested that maybe tonight was a first. How could she? With him? They always talked about him, and how lousy a husband he was, and yet she seemed ready, able and willing to lay with him. His whole body quaked with immense feelings of betrayal. The girls! He thought of them. He wondered if it would help if he drove to pick them up from Jenny's house. He had amazing gifts for them; even for Scarlett too. Oh, how he wished the evening had turned out in the way he had planned. He banged the desk. He turned off the music and sat in silence, trying not to think about what did or did not happen between Carl and Scarlett. He let his mind wander off. He looked out the window at the moonlit countryside. It reminded him of the picnic that he had with Kaela at the western shore of the Sea of Galilee. The green lawns and vistas of blooming exotic plants. How he now regretted running away from her. During those moments with her, he forgot about Zahara. She was the ideal replacement for Zahara. How she had readily showed him her own vulnerability, and enjoyed wallowing in Eli's conflicted depravity. But he ran away from her; to what end? He sat down feeling dejected.

He looked at the clock; 03:01am. He had dozed off. He knew exactly where he was. But he did not feel as mad as before. He had to face Scarlett, and talk about things. Dawn was approaching; the girls would come home.

CHAPTER FORTY-TWO

4 2 He opened the door slowly, not knowing what to expect. She sat on the bed, her eyes visibly sore from crying. She stood up as she used the bed throw to wipe her face. He stepped towards and put his hand on the roll of her waist. He hugged her. He uttered no word for a couple of minutes. Eventually, he whispered, "I am sorry, Scarlett. I do love you, babe. I always have."

"I am sorry too," she apologised too. Before she could say more, he released her gently from the hug, kissed her hair before pulling her to him, welding their bellies and loins. But she pushed back gently. "Wait, wait Eli," she said softly. "I am sorry for what happened. I know nothing will ever excuse that, but if it helps, nothing happened. He brought a bottle of wine, and he started talking about he missed his kids because Marion will not let him see them. And then he started talking about you being away and whether you were being faithful, and so on. Given where we were when you left, I felt vulnerable, but nothing happened. I swear on the girls' lives, Eli…"

"Shhh," Eli interjected. "I know, babe. My pride was hurt. It was not the welcome home I expected. Plus it was also the idea that you would have slept with him had I not gotten here just in time. Anyone else, but him! But it's ok. Nothing matters, ok, I love you. Do you know who I call for when I am having a nightmare? It does not matter where I am, it's always you that I call for. This is destiny; you are my destiny."

She was taken by his sweet words and his ready acceptance of her apology. She felt a surge of emotions. She reached down and grabbed the hardness of him. She gripped it and caressed its head. Her body juddered in anticipation. She pulled him to the bed.

Chapter Forty-Three

━━◦◦◦━━

43 For a long moment they sat in quietly in the dark holding hands. His mind shook as the heat of the regained passion lingered within his loins. The night was quiet, the day was truly dead, and everything else seemed far, far away. Scarlett pulled Eli towards him. She squeezed his hand as her other hand pulled his face closer to hers. She kissed him and his lips responded passionately. She felt enchanted within. All she could hear was his breathing, and it was like the sound of the sea. It gave her hope for their relationship. At long last, she could feel that sweet boy that she fell in love with many years ago. She could feel him opening up to her again; his love pouring out of the hidden caves of his heart. The image of her teen sweetheart overwhelmed her, and she fell in love again. The love descended into the hollow corners of her soul like rain into fountains. And they made love again.

The feeling was mutual. Eli was thankful that they had been afforded another chance to do it all again. A chance to go back to the way they were before, and better. Their rose-coloured past full of smiles and fond moments. He was grateful for the time away from home. Now they could both look beyond each day; beyond what they could see. He was ever so grateful. He squeezed her hand harder, and she squeezed back. It felt better than a dream for both of them.

Dawn lay grey on the chilling countryside, but the weather was not on top of the agenda. It felt good for both of them to wake up in each other's arms when daylight came. It was a brand new day, and for the first time in a very long time, they both felt and believed everything would really be okay. It seemed like their dragon days were truly gone. They both realised that maybe nothing was ever broken; perhaps, they had just been out of sync with each other at that time. It was a good thing they had not given up on each other. They just had to set a new direction, and not look back, and hope the gods above would finally give them their wedding bliss.

Chapter Forty-Four

44 Eli never felt more vindicated for his decision to take a sabbatical from his marriage. Seven months after his return, life could not be better. Bad days were gone. It had exceeded both their expectations. Eli had expected their newly found matrimonial harmony to be awkward, but everything seemed to fall in place. There now existed an unspoken bond full of mutual trust and understanding. Sex was now as natural and tranquil like any of their daily converses. Each night, they seemed to crawl back to each other, to where it all began when they were teenagers; to a place within themselves, a place only they knew. Eli looked forward to days turning into night so that he could be by her side, because then no one else was there but just the two of them. It seemed like those other times they told each other how much they loved them, they just did not show it enough or correctly.

The past was gone. Even the ghosts of Zahara were no more than simple memories of a life once shared.

CHAPTER FORTY-FIVE

—⁓⁓—

45 "Have you been to the tropics, lately?" the doctor asked as she took out a medical book from the shelf. "It is certainly not a cold or flu, and I would like to be extra cautious."

"No, he has not been anywhere, since he was last in Switzerland about a year ago," Scarlett said without looking at Eli who lay on the stretcher bed.

"His symptoms are synonymous with tropical nephropathies which are usually infective or toxic," the doctor explained.

"Which countries are in the tropics? Is Switzerland one of them? Or Italy? Didn't you go there one weekend, Eli?" she asked as she patted his shoulder.

"The tropics are parts of Africa, Asia, Central and South America and so forth; climates along the equator. Certainly not Switzerland or Italy. We need to do some more tests just to be rule out tropical diseases."

"What sort of diseases are we talking about doctor?" she asked again.

"There are toxic tropical nephropathies, which are often due to animal and insect poisons such as snake bites, scorpion stings, and so on, as well consumption of certain mushrooms and the djenkol bean," the doctor explained as she continued to flip through the book. "But I am more worried about infective nephropathies because these can cause renal infections, which would be of great concern given that you only have one kidney. You may get up and get dressed. I will order some blood tests and chest X-rays."

"What do you mean one kidney?" asked a flabbergasted Scarlett, again without looking at Eli. The doctor looked at Eli, and saw the awkward look on his face. Silence befell the room. Scarlett turned and looked at Eli, and motioned him to answer.

"Mrs Zwide, maybe you should give us some privacy?" It was more of an order than a request. Scarlett looked at Eli, and he looked down. She grabbed her bag and exited abruptly. "I will be in the car."

"Ok, Eli… can I call you Eli?" she asked and continued after he nodded, "So, what's going on? Your wife does not know you have just one kidney?" Again, Eli said no word, but simply shrugged his shoulders. The doctor grinned and said, "Men! I should have asked her to leave the room earlier, but I thought you were okay with her being there. Anyway, so have you been to the tropics?"

"Not the tropics as such, but sub-tropics, I think," he said and paused. "About a year ago, I spent about two and half months travelling in Israel."

"Was that after Switzerland?" the doctor asked. She knew the answer but she asked anyway.

"I travelled to France and then Israel and then back."
"Ok," she said sarcastically. "Let's get you down for some tests."

CHAPTER FORTY-SIX

<figure>ornamental divider</figure>

46 Scarlett did not look at Eli when he got into the car. "What did the doctor say?" she asked in an indifferent tone.

"I am sorry, Scarlett; I should have told you the truth," said Eli.

Still not looking at him, she asked again, "So, what did she say?"

"She has ordered some tests and referred me to a specialist," he responded. "I am sorry, babe," he said as he tried to take her hand but she pulled away.

"What do you have to be sorry about? It is your body, you do what you want with your organs, just do not lie about it."

"I needed some money for Justin's treatments, and there were some guys from Asia who paid me R120,000 for my kidney," he lied. "It was a stupid decision but I was lost, and mom and I were desperate for some cash to help out Justin. My mom was going to sell her house and so forth..."

"That's not the point, Eli" she interrupted him. "The point is you lied to me and made me look like a fool. You told me that the scar was from when your appendix was removed, and I gave you the benefit of doubt. What do you think I would have said had you told me that you had one kidney? Say I did not want to get back with you? Is that how much you value me as a person? That I would punish you for doing a noble thing for your brother?" She sneered as she looked at her watch. "Let's just go home."

"I am sorry," Eli apologised again as he turned on the engine.

"Whatever, Eli," she responded. "Now I doubt if the Justin kidney story is even true or whether you were really in Switzerland."

Eli did not respond, he just drove on quietly.

CHAPTER FORTY-SEVEN

47 "You punch like a girl," teased Eli.

"I am a girl, silly daddy," responded April.

"April, let's jump on him together," suggested Skye.

The girls climbed onto the couch and then jumped onto Eli's back. Eli basked in the moment of spending time with his little girls. He cast a glance at Scarlett, and she smiled and nodded approvingly before she said, "Enough girls, you know daddy is a bit poorly."

"It's alright," he responded. "I love my girls, and you know I love you, too."

"We love you, daddy," the girls said.

"They need to go tidy up their rooms anyway," she said. "Scuttle up the stairs, girls. First one back down gets sweeties; but you have to tidy up nicely."

As the girls hurried out of the room, Eli motioned Scarlett to come sit next to him. He put his arm around her, and kissed her on the cheek, and whispered, "Thank you for standing by me through and through, sweetheart. I do love you."

"No offence Eli, but you are starting to spook me now. Ever since you came back from the specialist, you have been… I don't know. I appreciate it, but I already know how much you love me, the girls. We are the ones who are blessed to have you," said Scarlett.

"I am sorry babe. Just been having the yearning to say what's on my mind, you know, just in case the sky falls down on us," he said as he softly squeezed her hand.

"I know, but you will be fine. Just don't spook us," she responded.

"Ok, but I can't help it at times, you know. I would rather say things and take them back, instead of drowning in regrets about things I never said. That's why I want you and the girls to know that if tomorrow starts without me, and I am not there to tell you these things…" Scarlett interrupted him. "Shhh," she said as she fondly kissed him.

"Oooh," yelled Skye. "Mum and dad K-I-S… uh, S. How does the song go, mummy?"

"I am not telling you. Did you finish tidying up?" asked Scarlett.

"Yes, I did. I did everything," she replied.
"Ok, go and get two sweets from the tin. Where is your sister?"

"Well, she is still tidying up, but she was playing with her teddy when I came down," reported Skye.

Eli got up and said, "I will go and help her. Do I also get sweeties?"

"How is my girl doing?" he asked as he gently knocked and entered April's bedroom.

"I am ok, daddy," she calmly said as he neatly lined up her soft toys.

"How come you did not try to finish first, and get the sweets?" Eli asked.

"Because Skye gets grumpy when she loses," she said. Eli was astounded by her response.

"That's good, honey, looking out for your sister. Well done. I am proud of you," he said as he hugged her and they both fell onto the bed. "But you still punch like a girl though," he taunted her some more. April sat on top of his belly, and punched him on the chest. They play-fought for a few minutes before finally finishing tidying up.

"That was a good punch, baby. That one really hurt, I am not pretending," he said as they walked down the stairs.

"Really daddy?" she asked. "Did it really hurt?"

"Yes, baby. I think I am going to need an ambulance," he joked as he brushed her hair with his fingers.

It was just after dinner, and Scarlett hummed softly in the kitchen as she loaded the dishwasher. Eli was sitting with the girls watching television. He had felt a bit woozy since dinner. He brushed it aside, and thought maybe he had eaten too much too quickly.

Then without warning, he gasped for air. He felt something unusual in the air, and then he felt cold; cold from nothing at all. His body shivered. He felt as if his lungs were filling with cold water; like he was drowning in icy cold waters.

"April," he muttered, "Get mummy."

"Mummy, mummy, something is wrong with daddy," she yelled. "Hurry mummy," added Skye.

"Eli, what's wrong?" asked Scarlett with fear and despondency in her voice.

"I am so cold," he muttered. "So cold; I feel like I am drowning."

She grabbed the phone, and as she dialled for emergency services, she yelled "Girls, go to the bedroom!"

"Which one?" asked Skye.

"It doesn't matter, just go. Now!" she said as she frantically dialled.

"Daddy, I am sorry I punched you," apologised April as she followed her sister into the hallway.

Chapter Forty-Eight

—◆—

48 It had been a long troublesome road for him. Even on the sunniest days of his life, he had always had an ache deep within. He had spent much of his lifetime looking for somebody to come and ameliorate life's burdens. But something felt different as he lay in the ambulance. He did not feel like a sojourner to nowhere anymore. He was happy that at least now Scarlett and the girls knew how much he really loved them. He had righted his many wrongs. Life or death, he was happy. Either way, he had left his demons and troubles in the past where they belonged.

"Dear God," he silently prayed. He had not prayed in a long time. There were many times he thought of praying but he felt he would just be lying to Him. In fact, he had not prayed since two days after meeting Kaela. "It has been a long troublesome road for me climbing up the rocky side of the mountain but please forgive for my shortcomings. Help me finally forgive my father for his own shortcomings. Forgive me for wandering into the ugly wilderness and leaving my girls alone; for not loving my wife better. I know my good and bad deeds were recorded but all I ask is that you continue to hold my girls' hands and guide them through life; for without you, they will be lost. The scripture says you can smite many generations for the sins of the forefathers but please spare my daughters your vengeance. Make the road easier for them than it was for me."

Eli opened his eyes and saw the paramedic sat next to him staring purposefully at him. The man was Arabic and in his mid-forties. "Are you a Muslim?" Eli muttered slowly. The man motioned him to keep quiet. "Just rest, sir. Do not strain yourself," the paramedic responded with a strong accent.

"I think I am about to meet my Maker. Please pray for me, if it's not too much bother," said Eli breathing heavily. The paramedic looked at his colleague, and the colleague shook his head, and whispered, "No religion matters with patients, Asif."

Asif sighed and put his hands to his face, and sighed stridently. He moved next to Eli, and took his hands, and began to pray in Urdu. His colleague muttered, "Don't do it, Asif. You could lose your job," but Asif kept on praying.

Eli's thoughts drowned in Asif's prayer. He felt nothing but silence. All he could hear was the beating of his own heart. He felt it gradually slow down. He felt icy cold water move up his body. He knew his time had come, and he was not scared but he was very sad for his little girls. He hummed tenderly the girls' favourite Christmas carol: *"O Come All Ye Faithful, Joyful and triumphant, O come ye, O come ye to Bethlehem..."*

CHAPTER FORTY-NINE

49 Scarlett paced about the hallway, constantly looking outside to see if her friend Savannah was there. She needed someone to look after the girls so that she could follow Eli to the hospital and be by his side. She muttered short prayers as she walked back and forth. Then the doorbell went.

"Oh, thank you Sav for doing this," she said as she opened the door but it was not Savannah at the door. "Hello," she said. "Sorry I thought you were my friend who is supposed to... Anyway, what can I do for you?"

"Hello," the stranger responded calmly. "I am looking for Eli."

"And you are?"

"My name is Kaela. I am a friend of his. I am in the area so I thought maybe I would pay him a short surprise visit."

"Kaela you said? He has never mentioned you..."

The sound of car approaching stopped her. "Oh, my friend is here. Sorry, Eli is not here, um, he has just been taken to the hospital. That's where I am headed."

"Oh my goodness, is he okay?" asked Kaela, but Scarlett did not respond.

"I am so sorry, Scarlett," apologised Savannah as she walked up to the door. "The traffic was horrendous, which was so unexpected this time of the day. Have you heard anything from the hospital?"

"No, nothing yet. I rang several times but they said he was not yet on the records. Anyway, thanks for coming, let me rush. You can move your car to the driveway once I am out. I will give you a call once I get to the hospital and let you know what time I will be back. Thanks again."

"Don't worry about rushing back. I will take the girls to bed."

Scarlett embraced the girls, and told them to be good. As she hugged Savannah, that is when she remembered Kaela.

"I am sorry, K... sorry, I can't remember your name. This is not a good time. I will tell Eli you passed through. Does he have your number?" she said as she paced to the car with Kaela following briskly behind.

"I am sorry to impose, but can I come with you to see him?" she asked tentatively. "Please? Besides, my hotel is in the city centre, that's where you are going, right?"

"Um... yeah, whatever. Let's go," answered Scarlett.

Scarlett hummed softly and tunelessly for the first few minutes. It was only when they got to the main road, that she cast a glance at Kaela. She noticed her beauty; a brown-skinned Arabic. Her hair was about the same length as hers, but more glossy.

"Sorry, what's your name again?"

"It's Kaela. I am so sorry for imposing, but Eli is an old friend so that I just thought I would say hello to him."

"Where do you know him from, then?" she quizzed.

"Um," hesitated Kaela. "We met when he was in Jerusalem."

"And where is this 'Jerusalem'?" she asked sarcastically.

"We met he was in Israel for a few weeks. I was sort of his tourist guide."

"Eli has never been to Israel or Jerusalem or whatever," said Scarlett genuinely mystified.

"Oh shit," thought Kaela. She remembered that Eli did mention that it was a secret trip. She silently cursed herself and twitched a bit.

"I am waiting for an answer, you know," said Scarlett visibly annoyed. "If you want to see my husband, I need you to be truthful for a start."

And she did.

"But nothing happened between us, honest," she lied. "Otherwise, I would not have had the nerve to come to your house. It was more of a therapeutic retreat for him. It was not about getting away or anything. He constantly talked about you, and the girls, and how he wanted to make things right."

Chapter Fifty

50 It took Eli a while to realise what had just happened. He looked down and saw his lifeless body being put onto a gurney. He saw Scarlett dashing into the room past the hoard of nurses. He saw them pulling her back as she wept, and as she grabbed the covered body on the gurney. He felt a new shade of sorrow. He was surprised that he could still feel that after he was dead. But he got an even bigger surprise when he saw a woman with a familiar face embracing Scarlett. He paused as he tried to recall where he knew the face from. Then it hit him. He panicked as he floated towards them. He tried to speak before realising they could not hear him. It was Kaela. What was she doing at his deathbed, and with his wife, he wondered. He watched Kaela lead Scarlett to the grief room. They sat down, still with Kaela's arm around Scarlett. He got closer to them. He tried to touch to Scarlett, and tell her he was truly sorry for all the hurt and lies, but he could not. He knew he had to go but decided he would stay for a bit longer.

The women just sat next to each other, occasionally exchanging glances but said no words. Every now and again, Kaela would get up and pace around the room before returning to the chair next to Scarlett, and each time softly rubbing her on the back.

"I am torn," confessed Scarlett without warning. She raised her head and cast a glance at Kaela. She was a stranger, but she wanted a hearty discussion with another woman or anyone who knew Eli. Kaela stared back with a look that said "How so?" Scarlett wiped the snort from her nose, and continued. "I feel like it's my fault because after I left him alone in South Africa with his dying little brother, it seems he packed ice around his heart. Maybe if I had stayed with him. But again, he is hurting me. Who had he become? You show up here with all these stories about him that I did not even know and probably would have never known had this not happened."

"I am sorry, Scarlett," she said. "But it's not your fault. It was never your fault. Eli's mind and heart were still trapped in a cage with that girl. He could never see past her. He tried to let her go, but she had a strong hold on him. I guess that is what happens if you love someone so strongly and so deeply. But for what it's worth, he loved you too; I guess he had a big heart. The trip he took was all about trying to make things right. He did it for you; for the family. If he had told you he was going away, would you have loved him still until he came back? How long before you phoned to say it was too late? He needed time, he needed space but it was not about you. It was for his sanity, your sanity, you know, for the girls' future. How were things after his return?"

"They were good, probably the best phases of our whole marriage. But he could have talked to me about his problems, his demons. I would have helped him; I would have loved him still."

Kaela hesitated as she carefully constructed the words in her head. "He knew about your brother, um, what your brother did to you and your sisters. But he loved you anyway, and he even confronted your brother, and I hope the problems stopped after that."

Scarlett was taken aback by the further revelation. How did he know?

Asif knocked on the door before entering. He had a middle-aged woman in a white coat with him. He stared at the two women, and said "Mrs Zwide?"

Scarlett moved her head slightly, and said "Yes? Are you the doctor? Can you tell me what happened?"

"I am sorry for your loss. No, I am not the doctor. I am a paramedic… I was with your husband in the back. Well, I will let the doctor speak to you first," he said signalling his female colleague to speak.

"I am Alison Parker, and I am one of the doctors who attended to your husband. We are very sorry for your loss," said the female doctor. She paused and watched Scarlett's reaction. "We are sending his body for a full post-mortem, but um, we believe he suffered multiple organ failure, including his kidneys… kidney."

Scarlett said nothing.
"Do you know what caused that?" asked Kaela.

"There are many factors that could cause that, but we would not want to speculate at this point."

"Could emotional stress cause that?" Kaela asked. Scarlett looked at her somewhat bewildered at her question.

"Um," hesitated the doctor. "Like I said there are many factors. I also understand he was having issues with his kidney, so it is best to wait for the post-mortem results, which hopefully should take 3-4 days. Once again, our heartfelt condolences to you."

"Thank you," Scarlett said finally, and then turned to Asif and asked, "Did he say anything when he was with you?"

"Yes, ma'am," responded Asif as he took out his notepad. "Just before we got here, he asked me to tell you 'No need to wonder what's been on my mind… nothing but you, and things and time. I am sorry for many things, but you know it has always been you. So, please don't regret me, don't regret us. Always remember the music and love that was in our teenage hearts; let that carry you farther that I ever could. You know I have always been scared of flying; so pray, I beg you sweet wife that I journey well.' That's all he said ma'am."

Asif and Alison turned to go. Scarlett forced a bland smile, and said feebly, "Thank you."

Asif glanced at her and said "It is not a problem, ma'am, and once again, I am so sorry. I know it's no consolation but he looked very much at ease, and he asked me to pray with him."

"Bastard!" she thought as she watched Asif and the doctor stride away, "He always knew what to say." She simpered wearily. He had remembered, and he had kept his sense of humour right to the death. "Things and time, huh?"

Kaela looked at Scarlett and realised she was feeling sorry for herself. Why shouldn't she? Widowed in her mid-thirties, and left with two young girls to raise by herself. She knew that at least money would not be an issue for Scarlett and the girls. Eli had once joked to her that he was worth more dead than alive, but she saw the fear in Scarlett's eyes. Kaela knew from experience that fear was a weak emotion. If Scarlett let it settle in her heart, it would eventually crawl into her soul and forever take away her inner peace. It would enslave her, put chains on her soul and whips on her back. She reached out and touched Scarlett's hand, and squeezed softly. Scarlett was slightly dazed by the unexpected touch of compassion from this woman she had met no more than two hours earlier, but she squeezed back.

Buoyed by Scarlett's appreciation of her kindness, Kaela continued, "Let us trust the past to the mercy of God, the present to His love, and the future to His providence."

Kaela was not even sure what that meant, but she had heard it somewhere, and it certainly felt like the right thing to say. Scarlett sniffled as tears continued to pour out of her baggy eyes.

"It will be alright, Scarlett," Kaela added. "It will hurt like hell, but the life goes on; the show must go on as they say. It has to go on for you and your girls. Come on, we have a funeral to plan."

Throughout their time together, Eli had always had a way with words; he had always known what to say to her. "He always said you might be around tomorrow, but there is no guarantee that your dreams and hopes will be. How so true," Scarlett said as she let tears and snort smear her make-up. Kaela knew that all too well, so she nodded quietly as Scarlett continued, "He was my dream and hope. I loved him."

"Me too," Kaela said instinctively and regretted it as soon as they words left her lips. Scarlett looked at Kaela saw the hurt in her eyes, and realised how much they were going to need each other.

Eli watched the two women saunter dejectedly out of the hospital. He felt more than sadness for them. He felt grave compunction for all the things he had not made right with his wife. But he did tell her when they got married that if he ever changed in time, it was because of his troublesome past. He had hoped that Scarlett understood that they were not just words. The past changed him. He kept staring at them as they walked towards the car park, but he knew it was time to go.

As Scarlett sat in the car disconsolately, she could not help but pray for Eli. It was the only thing she was taught to do in times like these. "Faithful Father in heaven, be with my Eli. As he journeys beyond the blue skies, may the angels help lead the way. May our prayers shine on his soul and keep him safe. Please grant him eternity, and may his mum and brother be there to greet him as he passes the gates into the tunnel's light. Keep him safe for me, oh dear Lord. Amen."

CHAPTER FIFTY-ONE

5 1 Eli expected it to be different. He expected a white light to shine through the clusters of white and golden-yellow roses. He expected the mood to be mellow, but he found himself walking through a hall of mirrors with flickering lights. Some sections were misty and grey, and were lit by many candles. He saw his mum and Justin waiting at the end of the hallway. Justin yelled, "Eli! I have been waiting for you for so long. Welcome brother." Eli looked at his little brother. He looked well. He had no sign of the disease that had ravaged his body right from the day he was born. Eli turned to his mum. She looked very distressed and somewhat in a poignant mood but her body looked nothing she did the last days of her life. She looked back at Eli, and shook her head disapprovingly. "You should not have come, Eli. It was not your time. It does not matter anyway, let's go."

"Where are we going, ma? What is this place?" he responded.

Justin grabbed Eli's hand, and enthusiastically said, "Yes, bro, let's go. I have waited for this for a long time."

"I am sorry, ma, but I need to find Zahara," said Eli as he turned and stared back at the hallway with flickering lights. He listened to the echoes of cries for mercy, intermittently broken by whispers of love.

"No, Eli. Let her go. This is the path that leads to eternal peace," she pleaded.

"I am sorry, ma, but hell or high water is what I promised her. No one ever loved the way I love her. I have to have her. I promised her my love to death and beyond."

He paused and bent down and kissed Justin on the forehead, and whispered, "I am sorry, little bro. Go on without me, I will find you. I promise."

"Don't do this, Eli. I need you," begged Justin. "I have been waiting for you for a long time. I have seen the other side. It's much better; there are birds singing, strangers holding hands, roses blooming, bright shining lights, no dark clouds at all, just bright rainbows… please, Eli. This is where you belong. This is our peace at last, brother; come on."

"He is right, Eli," added his mum. "This is where we belong. Don't worry, your good outweighs the bad, and that's all that matters."

"I am sorry," Eli said. "I really am, but I made a promise."

The End

Page 6 contains an excerpt from a song written by Bill Monroe and published by Unichappell Music Inc (BMI).

ABOUT THE AUTHOR

Mac Muzvimwe is a chartered surveyor in his mid-thirties, born in Zimbabwe, but living and working in the south west of England. Writing is a hobby he picked up in his teens, and he has written several short stories which he self-published in 2009. Demons in Cold Water is his first novel. He is married and has two young boys.

Printed in the United States
By Bookmasters